Clara's Curse

ALSO BY TARA L. THOMPSON

Before I Say I Do

Divided Souls

Clara's Curse

Tara L. Thompson

ISBN-978-1-7375673-0-1

ISBN- 978-1-7375673-1-8

Dedicated with many thanks and love to

Diann Thompson (my mother)

And

Glenda Gathers (my aunt)

Thank you for your strength, power, and voice.

In Memory of
Clara Bell Thompson
Georgia Mae Davis
Mary E. Shields
Frances Davis DeBerry
Edward Scott
Minnie Scott
Laquanya Hayden
You all touched my life in many ways.
I love and miss you dearly.

Acknowledgments

Two years ago, in the midst of writing Clara's Curse I gave up. I was heartbroken, defeated, and depressed. My relationship had just ended and I had buried four family members in the span of three months. I had no desire to write and my days of being an author were over. However, during those times God spoke to me the most. After having numerous signs from God, he came to me in a dream. I was alone in a dark room sitting on the floor. No one was around me and I could hear a voice repeatedly calling my name. I looked down and in my hands was a pen and a piece of paper. I had this same dream for the next three nights. Finally, I woke up after the fourth night of having that same dream and begin to write again. Immediately a calmness came over me that I had not felt in months. I sat at my computer writing and crying. That day I wrote five of the best chapters I had ever written. God has showed me time and time again even if I give up on myself, he never gives up on me. I thank him for the strength to write Clara's Curse and also for my gift that I continue to share with the world.

Special thanks to my editors, Mrs. Barbara Joe Williams and Ms. Latoya Smith. Thank you both for making me dig deeper and for realizing how important this book is to me. Another thanks to my proofreader, Ms. Sylvia Thomas. Thank you each for all your hard work on this project.

Thank you to my fans, supporters, friends, and family. Thank you for encouraging me, supporting me, and reminding me that you all were waiting on my next novel. So many days your words made me push forward and keep going. Special thanks to the ladies of The Sip 6 for the sisterhood and all the amazing ideas. As always, a big thank you to my parents, sisters, my daughter, and my girls! Thank you all and I love you so much!

To my readers, I promise I will never make you wait another five years for a novel. Thank you for still being here. I will always give you my absolute best!

Love and Blessings,

Tara L. Thompson

This is my story, and this is my curse.

Generational curses are described as misfortunes or evils that pass through a family from ancestor to ancestor over a span of time.

The vicious cycle can begin with a great-grandmother and travel from grandmother to mother and daughter, each experiencing the same plague.

However, generational curses can be broken…

Prologue

ClaRina

I was a hypocrite. Hypocrisy flowed through my body as if it were the only substance that willed me to stay alive. It seeped through my pores with every breath I took and erupted from my mouth with every word that passed between my lips. My name should have been ClaRina "Hypocrite" Kendall Faulk since that one word represented my entire existence and was exactly what had brought me to this moment.

I sucked in two quick breaths and slowly exhaled to slow the beating of my heart. Lifting my shaking hand, I rubbed my eyes, smearing fresh warm blood all over the right side of my face. Sweat dripped from my new pixie cut and found its way to the corners of my eyes. Between the mixing of both body fluids, it was impossible to see clearly. I was almost at the point of losing my mind, but now I imagined things as well. I felt like the young boy in the movie *The Sixth Sense*. His words crept from my mouth and were released as a mere whisper, "I see dead people."

My living room was dark, except for the moonlight shining through the slits of my blinds. Glancing over to my right, which was the only dimly lit corner of the room, I hoped the person who had appeared had vanished just as quickly. However, I was not that lucky. She was as evident as the half-dead body that lay at my feet. My grandmother, or Mother Clara as we called her, sat in her once favorite red oak wooden rocking chair, calmly moving back and forth. Draped over her large body was the black and white striped housecoat she wore when I was a child. A blank expression was frozen on her face and her long gray hair, which was always pinned up in a bun, was in disarray.

However, her confused demeanor wasn't what almost made my knees buckle. In my grandmother's lap rested a two-by-four. The large piece of lumber was drenched with blood that dripped onto my hardwood floors.

"Mother Clara?" I asked, whispering.

She didn't stop rocking, nor did she look at me. She didn't even pause to acknowledge my presence. The bright red liquid continued to steadily fall from the wood. I attempted to call her name again, but the words were bound in my throat. My hands were soaked from the perspiration and blood. I wiped them on my blue-pinstriped suit pants. But no matter how hard I tried; I couldn't get them clean.

"It's not going anywhere," a voice from the opposite side of my living room called out.

I peered through the darkness where the words had traveled from and saw her—my mother. Again, I was seeing dead people.

"Mom?" my voice was barely audible at this point.

She stood in the corner and smiled at me. She wore a simple black dress on her slender frame. As always, she looked beautiful and fancy. Her medium-length tresses were cut in a bob, and she seemed peaceful. A peace that was not at all parallel to the mother I had known.

"Mom, is that really you? Ruth Ann?"

She smiled again. As her grin slowly transformed into a scowling frown, I noticed what was in her hand. She looked down, gripped the handle of a silver pistol, and then looked back up at me. I shook my head. My mind was playing tricks on me. The gun she held in her hands was the exact gun I clutched in mine.

"You are me," my grandmother and mom said together.

"No!" I screamed, shaking my head, and dropping the pistol to the floor. "No, no, no!"

My grandmother stood from her chair and finally looked at me. She and my mom began to move toward me; Mother Clara with her bloody two-by-four, and my mom with her gun. They pointed both objects at me.

"You are us," they said in unison.

Their words sent a chill through my body, and I couldn't stand up any longer. I fell to my knees, landing in a sea of blood.

"I'm not!" I cried out. "Please, God, I'm not like them," I pleaded as if the Master above could hear me. Even if He could, I doubted He would pay my pleas any attention after what I had done.

"You are us," rang in my ears over and over again as I buried my face in my hands and cried.

Moments passed, and the room fell silent. My tears subsided. I looked around for my mother and grandmother, but they were now gone. The only person left in the room with me was Harold. My husband's lifeless body was lying on the floor in front of me.

His head faced me, and fresh blood streamed from his mouth. His soulless eyes were still open, staring at me as if to ask why.

"Oh, God! I am them," I said as the realization of what I had done sunk in. Just then, even though they were gone, I still heard the voices of the two women who just had stood in front of me. And since I was more like them than I ever wanted to admit, I would do exactly what they would have done at this moment.

I picked up my gun from the floor, regained just enough strength to point it at Harold, and pulled the trigger once more.

"Even if I hadn't killed you, you were going to die anyway."

Chapter 1

Ruth Ann

1953

Tonight, would be my last night fighting him off of me. It would be my last night weeping and begging for my life. This night would be the final time I had to scream for help. Tonight, would be the end of my existence in this wretched country town.

I buried my head into the chest of the only man who truly loved me. The crisp September night caused me to snuggle closer to him. My brother Bobby, or Bo, as we affectionately called him, held me softly and made sure he did not squeeze me too tight. My heart was in pieces; my entire body was still raw from the previous night's battle. The right side of my face was bruised, and my left eye was almost swollen shut. Even the smallest touch made my petite frame cringe and ache in pain. I could not bear the torture any longer, and he knew it.

"Gal, git way. And I mean far way. Go on up yonder to that New York City where Auntie Mae is. Just git now!" My brother's powerful rustic baritone voice was laced with such a deep Southern drawl. One could never mistake that it originated from the lowest parts of the South. His muscular arms covered my body for a few more seconds. Bo had been my safe haven ever since I could remember. He protected me the best he could. However, after last night, we knew the next time I was in danger might be my last time.

He broke our embrace and gently pushed me away. The hurt that settled on his face was evident each time he looked at me. "Now listen," Bo said, lifting my chin so he was staring squarely into my eyes. "I dun saved up nuff for yo' train ticket and ya to live off fo' at least two months."

We were huddled up outside the train station in Columbia, South Carolina, an hour away from my hometown, Timmonsville.

It was almost midnight, and the wind whipped around us, whistling for my immediate departure as well. The train would be boarding soon, and time was not an ally now. I longed to savor just a few more minutes with my brother.

Bo had snuck me out of the house and needed to get back before our parents realized we were missing. I shook my head as defeated tears dropped from my eyes. I pushed a few strands of hair from my face and smoothed it back into the ponytail holder that was barely keeping it together. Knowing that Bo detested tears, I sniffed and tried to get them under control. "Never show 'em you hurtin', sis," my brother repeated to me every single day.

I finally failed at my attempt, and the tears continued to pour down. Bo would be the only one I missed. He was seven years older than me, and we shared a bond I did not have with my other four brothers and sister.

As we stood outside the station, he was again doing all he could to keep me out of harm's way, even if that meant sending me to go live with my aunt in another state.

"What 'bout my babies, Bo?" I managed to ask through my tears. I had just turned nineteen and given birth to my second daughter, Gwendolyn, four months ago. My oldest daughter, ClaRina, was almost four.

They had to know I loved them and were the reason I was leaving this evil town, and this wicked family. I prayed one day they would understand the choice I was left to make. There was no other alternative for me. It was either leave or die.

"Ni, ya ain't gotta worry 'bout dem babies. I'll take care of 'em. Just like I looked after you, Imma look after 'em."

"I'm gone come back for 'em," I sniffed. "I promise, Bo. I'm comin' back fo' my girls. I love 'em."

"I know, Ruthie, I know. But fo' now ya gotta git. I ain't gone bury my sister, so jus git." Bo handed me the ticket and money and pointed toward the doors of the train station.

Bo calling me Ruthie caused a slight smile to creep across my puffy face. That was his nickname for me whenever he comforted me. There had been so many occasions during my life that my older brother had to console me.

"I love you, Bo," I said, giving him another quick embrace. As I let him go for the second time, I saw a single tear roll down his cheek.

Bo's charcoal skin and bloodshot eyes made him look like a heartless menace rather than the peaceful soul he really was. Although he was dressed in a pair of dingy blue jean overalls he had worn earlier while working in the fields, he was still handsome. A humble smile stretched across his face that only I was privy to, and the jokes he often made took my mind off of the repugnance seen daily. I often called him my gentle giant.

Bo straightened his shoulders, cleared his throat, and pointed again toward the train. I closed my thin, black-tattered jacket and picked up my plastic bag filled with the only clothes I could grab from the house. I rushed toward the station, so I would not miss my train. Once I got to the door, I paused and contemplated if I could really leave. If I remained, it would only be for my girls. But staying would mean more days and nights succumbed to torture and molestation. Not getting on that train would mean more bruises and sores. Going back to that house would mean me wanting to take my own life just to escape it all.

I did not want to abandon ClaRina and Gwen in a place I was running from. The same suffering I had endured, I could not imagine falling upon them, too. But what other choice did I have? I had no more fight left in me.

I looked back at my older brother one final time. My mind was eased somewhat from knowing that Bo would be there for my girls. I prayed that my daughters would remain untouched due to their young age. My plan was to come back and get them before they reached the same age I did when my abuse began. I had full faith that Bo would make sure they were safe until my return.

Bo's hard-chiseled face was covered with worry. If Mother or Father knew he helped me flee, no telling what they would do to him. Crossing his arms over his chest, he nodded, instructing me to go inside. I did as I was told, unaware of what the future would hold for me, not sure of what I would do when I arrived in New York. And completely oblivious to the fact that when I looked back at my favorite brother, Bo, it would be the last time I saw him alive.

Chapter 2

ClaRina

1965

"I can't believe we gotta go to school wit' dese crackas!" Gwen folded her arms across her chest and stomped her foot, invoking a cloud of dust upon her freshly shined navy-blue Mary Janes. Lace hung from her frilly off-white socks, and the dirt she just awoken from under her feet would surely make them look even more dingy. The last thing I wanted was to have a snobby kid picking at her because of her dirty socks. She had enough to fret about today.

"You know, Mother gone git you if she hears you talkin' like dat." I glanced at the screen door to make sure Mother Clara was not in earshot of our conversation.

"I don't care, Ri Ri! I don't wanna go!" Gwen protested, stomping her foot once more. Again, I glanced at her socks that, as I thought, looked a shade darker.

Gwen never called me by my full name, ClaRina. She always addressed me as Rina. However, the times that she required me the most I was Ri Ri to her. She was the only one that called me Ri Ri, and in those moments, I knew I had to do everything I could to take care of her. In return, I shortened her name from Gwendolyn to Gwen.

"Stop whining ni!" I glared at my little sister. "We ain't got no choice. Just don't look scared or cry. We gonna get through this. I ain't gone leave ya."

Gwen tugged on the sleeves of her sky-blue blouse that once belonged to me and stared at the ground. "I'm no baby! I ain't gone cry, Rina." She sniffed as tears began to form in the corners of her eyes.

I slid over from where I was sitting on our grandmother's porch and put my arm around my little sister. "Come on, sis, ya know they can't do nothin' to the Kendall girls!" I joked.

I wasn't sure if my feeble attempt at trying to cheer her up would work, but that was all I could offer at the moment. "And I'll make sho' I sneak ya something sweet after supper if ya don't cry. I saw Mother Clara cannin' preserves late last night. No way you don't want no hot biscuits and delicious pear preserves."

Gwen looked up at me, smiled, and wiped the tears that were slowly making their way down her face with the back of her hand. Her sweet tooth and the vision of our grandmother's fruit preserves were much greater than her fear of a new school, so I figured that would halt her tears.

She also thought she was prettier than most girls in our small town of Timmonsville. That was attributed to her sandy cinnamon complexion and thick brownish-red hair that fell past her shoulders. Our uncles joked that her dad was a white man who used to creep around the house at night to see our mom. But we knew that Gwen's father was just ol' high yellow Percy who lived down the street and around the corner from us with his wife and seven kids. Due to her already self-proclaimed beauty, she definitely would not want anyone to witness her weeping.

I turned my focus back down the gravel road to see if the school bus was anywhere in sight. The sweltering August sun awoke with a vengeance and stirred around even more anxiety in me. Not only did I have to console Gwen, but I also had to pretend as if I was not frightened.

Even though the sun suspended in the sky's motive, was to brighten our day, no sunshine and luminous rays could remove the dark cloud that hung over our heads. Today was one day that we would remember for the rest of our lives.

The decision of Brown v. Board of Education had passed a few years ago but was never implemented into the school systems of South Carolina until now. The ruling that would forever change our lives stated we could not continue to be educated with only black kids since it was deemed unequal.

We were now forced to go to school with white children who despised us just because of our skin color. My previous high school, Dennis High, was the first one in the county to enforce this law and was forced to shut down. I was beginning my senior year of high school; however, this was Gwen's freshman year. I felt an overwhelming amount of pity for her. Not only was she starting high school already fearful of being in an older environment than middle school, she was also made to do that with kids who truly thought we were inferior to them and felt that we were not worthy to be in their presence, let alone be educated with them.

I dreaded going to our new school, too, but there was nothing we could do about it. So, we had to put on our brave faces and get through it. One step at a time. One hour at a time. One day at a time.

The monstrous school bus, stained with caked-on mud and a faded yellow paint job as old as our grandmother, slinging dirt and gravel as it barreled toward us, interrupted my thoughts.

I watched it bulldoze down Thomas Street to pick us up and then carry us off into the unknown. Wilson High School would be our new school, and we were unsure of what would take place. At the moment, I would have given anything just to go back to my old school with my old teacher and familiar friends.

"Come on," I ordered, standing, and brushing the dirt from the back of my khaki pants. Because I was the oldest, I was afforded one new outfit. And since it was the first day of school, no better day to wear my fitted bell-bottom khakis and a yellow button-down blouse.

It was nothing fancy, but I didn't get to enjoy new clothes all the time. So, this basic outfit meant the world to me. My thick jet-black afro was picked out to the highest form. I suddenly rethought, displaying all my hair glory and drawing more attention to myself. Unlike Gwen, my dark chocolate skin tone was way more intimidating than hers. Unfortunately, as I watched the school bus come closer, it was too late to change anything about my hairstyle now.

"We gonna make it," I assured Gwen. I tightened my grip on her hand as the bus stopped in front of us.

My heart sank deeper into the pit of my stomach once the doors of the rusty bus squeaked open, and Mr. Ralph, the bus driver, sneered at us. He was the most revolting human being I had ever come within mere inches of touching. He was more terrifying than Mr. John, who ran the corner store in the middle of town. Mr. John, or lizard lips as we secretly dubbed him because of his slimy mouth that resembled the creepy reptile's, would rush us to get what we came for and leave his store quickly. We rarely encountered white people since the schools had been segregated, and we did not get to go into town with Mother Clara often. Being this close to an unsavory man was a first. His beady red eyes, soiled blond hair, and corroded yellow teeth reminded me of why I feared and loathed white people so much.

The abhorrent sight of the buttons of his greasy indigo oxford shirt, holding on for dear life as his potbelly rested on the steering wheel, made me want to regurgitate the breakfast I had just consumed. I imagined standing in front of him and expelling the sausage and grits that Mother Clara had served us right in his grungy face.

Mr. Ralph turned up his nose at Gwen and me, and then stared straight ahead. I guided Gwen in front of me to protect her. My legs wobbled as I climbed the three stairs. I slid past Mr. Ralph and nearly choked on the powerful smell of tobacco smoke surrounding him.

"Hurr' up, damn it!" he insisted.

"Niggers!"

"Monkeys!"

"Go back to Africa!" rained down on us from the front, back, and sides of the bus.

The reprehensible words assaulted us, piercing our souls, and weighing us down, making it almost unbearable to move our feet. I placed both of my hands on Gwen's shoulders, squeezed tightly, and directed her down the aisle, which seemed like it would never end. As the white children continued to glare and scream at us, we realized quickly that we were the only black kids on the bus.

We were halfway down the walkway, still searching for a seat when I finally saw the last one at the back of the bus was empty. I practically pushed Gwen the rest of the way down the aisle. This seat was our savior—a small escape from the jeers and callous words.

Finally, we were at the back. Once I laid eyes upon our salvation, I wanted to burst into tears. The one seat the kids had left for us was covered with repulsive mucus-filled saliva on the back and bottom cushions.

"What we gone do, Ri Ri?" Gwen asked, grabbing my hand on her shoulder as the taunts and slurs continued.

"We don't want yo' kind here!"

"Porch monkeys!"

"Coons!"

"Go home!"

"Tar babies!"

The insults continued to come at us. I gathered up all the strength I had and tried to think of something fast. I reached into the brown bag carrying my lunch and unwrapped the paper towel covering the ham sandwich Mother Clara had fixed for me. I wiped off a tiny portion of the seat, just enough for me to sit down.

"Sat y'all black asses down back dere!" Mr. Ralph screamed.

"Sit on my lap, sister," I coaxed, pulling Gwen down on top of me. She looked horrified and was trying her best not to cry.

I closed my eyes and said a silent prayer that she would be able to make it through the day. Little did I know, this ordeal on the bus was merely the beginning.

Chapter 3

Gwen

I hopped off of the bus and ran halfway down Mother Clara's gravel driveway. Not caring that I had on short pants, I fell to the ground into a praying position. The pain of the rocks piercing into my skin was nothing compared to what I had undergone for the last eight hours.

"Girl, git up and come on 'fo Mother git us!" Rina yelled, disappearing into the house.

I didn't move just yet. I had to thank God for getting me through the most horrific day of my fourteen years on this earth. From the dreadful bus ride to walking down the halls and having kids throw paper, food, or whatever they could grab at me, I was ecstatic to be home. The view of my grandmother's house almost brought tears to my eyes. No matter how horrendous it was inside this home, it did not compete with the awfulness inside that school building.

I got up, dusted myself off, and ran toward the house so I could get started on my chores. As I walked through the doorway, I saw

Rina sweeping out the kitchen. Upon entering the front door of our small white-bricked house, we walked straight into the living room, where a seedy crimson carpet covered the floors. No matter how much Rina or I cleaned the worn carpet, it always had the same grimy look to it.

A narrow hallway led from the living room to the kitchen, where Rina was cleaning up. On the other side of the kitchen, the second hallway led to three bedrooms. Rina's and my jobs were to keep the kitchen, living room, and our bedroom clean. Almost the entire house was left for us to make sure no dust, trash, or leftover food was scattered around or anything out of place.

"She outside; ya better hurry," Rina whispered, pointing at the back door. I stared at Rina and thought about how she had protected me earlier on the bus.

I was so afraid and close to tears while watching those blue-eyed devils mock us. But like always, my sister had been there for me.

"Gal, go!" Rina yelled, snapping me out of my thoughts.

Rushing so as not to get caught by Mother Clara, I dashed to the bedroom that Rina and I shared and threw my books on my bed. Our bedroom was much like the rest of the house, desolate and cold. Two twin beds covered in beige quilts crafted by Mother Clara were propped across from each other in our miniature white-walled room. At one time, the room we slept in was shared by my mom, Ruth Ann, and her sister, Florence. Now, unfortunately, it was Rina's and my domain. I had only about five minutes to change out of my school clothes into my work clothes. Unlike the white kids who switched into play clothes after school, there was no play at our house. All we did was go to school and come home to work.

I walked out of my room and peeked around the corner just as my grandmother Clara marched into the kitchen. Mother Clara, or Mother as we called her because she was raising us instead of our real mom, was fifty-two years old with the power of a sumo wrestler and the three-hundred-pound weight to match. Her strength and size were regularly used to whip my sister and me for misbehaving or not moving quickly enough to do the things she required.

Mother Clara's massive hands were bruised from constant work in the fields, but that never stopped her from delivering vicious punches and slaps to us. Her stoic, commanding bronze-colored face only presented us with a frown and disapproving stares from day to day.

The only word I could think of whenever I looked at my grandmother was hard. Her face was hard, her hands were hard, and her love, if she loved us at all, was hard. Honestly, I believed she only tolerated us because she was tasked with the burden of raising us.

Day in and day out, she loomed over me like a grotesque demon, bellowing orders and constantly reminding me that I would never be worth shit, just like my mother. I would in no way ever forgive my mom for leaving my sister and me here in this hellhole while she lived and enjoyed life in New York. Her life was a dream while ours was a nightmare.

"Gal, git yo' ass out der and help Lee!" My grandfather's voice rocked the entire house. He stuck his head in the backdoor to make his demand and disappeared just as quickly.

Grandpa Henry was a broad-shouldered husky, chestnut-toned man, who stood about seven feet tall. Intimidation and fright embodied him, causing most people to step back two or three feet before addressing him. I did not know who I despised more, him or Mother Clara. However, he was ten times as vile as Mother, if that was possible. I did my best to stay out of both of their ways. He rarely addressed me unless it was to tell me to go work in the fields.

I ran outside and searched my grandparents' land for Uncle Lee. Grandpa Henry owned a little over thirty acres of land, stretching clear across Thomas Street on both sides and ending at Uncle Theodore's—his brother—house at the far end of the road. Rolling pea-green fields hidden by high stalks of cotton provided my family with the means to survive.

Rina and I detested the fluffy white balls surrounded by thorns that often-left scars on our hands since we were the main ones assigned to pick the annoying objects. Grandpa Henry was a proud man. He worked hard for his land and believed in keeping what belonged to him in the Kendall name. He cherished his property and every piece of cotton that grew from it.

Among the fields, ten acres of land were cleared off for my grandparents' house. A half-mile down the road, from where we resided, was home to Grandpa Henry's beloved night club, The Kendall Social Club.

After a few minutes, I finally spotted Uncle Lee in the fields across from the club. The Kendall Social Club was widely known all over the town of Timmonsville and surrounding areas. It was commonly called the "hot spot" on Friday and Saturday nights.

The minute silver tin building that appeared to be just another house or storage area was opened by my great-grandfather, Otis, many years ago. It was nothing fancy, but the power it bestowed was more valuable than any other lavish club in the entire state of South Carolina. My grandfather and uncles owned and operated the club now since my great-grandfather was no longer living.

Since our family's night club was the only one in our town, if one wanted to party or have a few drinks, one would usually end up at The Kendall Social Club. The club was accessible every night of the week.

A few people frequented the club during the week; however, it was filled to capacity on the weekends. Men and women, ranging from twenty-five to seventy, crammed the building, smoking, drinking, playing pool, and dancing. Because of the club's popularity, the Kendall name held a lot of weight in our small town. Everyone knew our family, and no one dared mess with anyone carrying the last name Kendall.

"Stop starin' off in space and git one of dem shovels, chile." Uncle Lee's raspy voice broke up my thoughts. Hopefully, the night would swiftly fall upon us. After a day like today, all I wanted to do was take a hot bath and get in my bed.

•••

"Yo' sweet ass gittin' round, Gwen," Uncle Lee slurred as I headed toward the house. I did not comment and refused to turn around, but I felt his eyes watching my every step. I quickened my pace so that he wouldn't catch up with me.

Ever since I turned fourteen a few months ago, his salacious remarks were becoming more frequent. Rina warned me about him and promised she would protect me. As long as I had my sister in my corner, I knew I would be safe. I slid open the rickety sliding glass door on the back of the house and an open hand on my right cheek welcomed me in.

"Ain't I tell ya to git in here an hour ago?" Mother Clara snarled.

Her sudden slap twirled me around and landed me on my knees. She hit me so hard I couldn't answer her question. All I could do was grab the side of my face and hold back the tears destined to come soon. I pulled myself back up on my feet and stood to face Mother. She stood in front of me, waiting for an answer, but daring me to talk back to her. I steadied myself, and another slap found my left cheek due to me not responding to the question asked when I first walked into the house. This time, a high screech escaped my lips. My obscure cry was again greeted with another shallow hand to my face.

I ran past the darkness of my grandmother and bolted for my room. I fell on my bed. The screams I had successfully held in only a few moments ago were relinquished into my pillow all at once.

Over my wails, I felt my sister tugging on my arm. "Gwen, hush up now," Rina whispered. "You know that cryin' ain't gone do nuthin but piss Mother off mo'. Hush it up ni. I can get ya some sweet bread if ya quiet down."

When I heard Mother Clara's shoes sliding across the floor, my crying suddenly stopped.

It would be moments before she was in my room with her heavy hands pounding down on me. I braced myself for her to appear in the doorway like a dense dark cloud before a massive thunderstorm. I closed my eyes, awaiting her arrival. My body was stiff.

After a few seconds, I was gasping for air from holding my breath without realizing I was doing so. I opened my eyes, expecting to see Mother, but there was no one there.

Rina wasn't even in the room anymore. I sat up on my bed and gently massaged my stinging face. My room was the best place for me to be right now, away from danger. I laid back down and closed my eyes again, hoping that sleep would take away the pain.

Chapter 4

Beatrice

"Git it off me!"

As soon as I heard my mother's familiar voice, followed by a ghastly scream, I ran into my hiding place. They wouldn't be able to find me here. As many times as I had hidden in this closet, I knew I would be safe, at least for a little while. I didn't want my mother to know where my secret place was, so I would sneak out once the yelling and fighting stopped. I closed my eyes and longed to be somewhere else—other than this apartment. In times like these, I even yearned to be with my sisters, ClaRina and Gwen. I never wished to be with them except for days like this. Honestly, I didn't even know or care for them much. And since I didn't know them, I didn't trust them. Still, no matter what my sisters went through, it had to be better than hiding in the closet twice and sometimes three times a week. And I was almost certain they ate every day. For me, eating twice a day was a luxury and only meant my mom had gotten her food stamps. Perhaps the only reason she kept me with her was to get food stamps and some extra money each month. The money she and my dad argued about all the time. Exactly like they were doing right now.

I had gotten home from school about an hour ago and found some stale barbeque potato chips in the cabinet. I was huddled in my small room and had just finished my snack when I heard my mom come through the front door fussing with my dad behind her. The battling continued. Once I heard something shatter against the wall, I knew it was time to go to my private sanctuary.

"Ray, I ain't giving you no mo' damn money!" my mom shouted. "Don't ask me no goddamn mo'!"

The sobbing that followed meant my father had hit my mother. As the tears streamed down my face, all I thought about was getting away. After all the times I had witnessed my parents fighting, I never got used to seeing my mom with a bloody nose or black eye. As I listened to her screams and howls, I was convinced that both injuries would soon be visible.

"Bitch, don't make me hurt ya!" My father's voice rattled the entire apartment and caused me to scoot further in the corner of my closet. I slid as far back as I possibly could and prayed. I didn't know much about God and asking Him to help me, but I figured there had to be someone out there who could come to my rescue.

"Stop!" my mother yelled right before I heard another big boom.

My mother, Ruth Ann, was not the nurturing or caring type. As a matter of fact, she never expressed that she loved me. The only time I sensed she felt some fondness for me was when she cooked now and then. Every so often, on a Saturday morning, the aroma of bacon drifted into my room, waking me up and causing me to be delighted that I was in this place with her. It was a wonderful day when I smelled food.

"Bea, come eat!" she playfully sang in her highest Soprano voice.

I skipped into the kitchen and sat at the table in front of a plate full of bacon, pancakes, and eggs. I looked at my mother's chocolate skin, jet-black hair hanging past her shoulders, broad nose, plump lips, and imagined she was different. I envisioned her being comforting and expressing to me every day how much I was loved. Unfortunately, that was not my reality. She wouldn't say much to me while we ate breakfast.

But just being around her when she was calm was enough to soothe some of the rough days. Then there were times, after she and my dad fought, that she would come in my room, sit on my bed, and ask how I was doing. She always ended those conversations with the same advice, "Don't trust nobody." So, I remembered her words and did not have faith in anyone, not even her.

However, during those morning breakfasts and evening visits, I felt as if she liked me or at least had some sort of spot in her heart for me. But most of the other times, a burden was all I appeared to be, and that she was forced to be responsible for me.

I was only ten, but I was nothing like the girls my age at school or even around my neighborhood. They didn't have to take care of themselves like I had to do. My mom worked twelve and thirteen-hour shifts as a certified nursing assistant at the Angel Crest Hospital a few blocks from our apartment. I woke myself up and got dressed for school every day. I fixed my own meals whenever there was food in the house. If I didn't want to go to school, I didn't have to since my mother never checked to see if I really went. But every day, I got up because I wanted to be better than her. I didn't want to work as hard as she had to and still have nothing. I wanted more than that.

"I know you got mo' money than this!" my dad's high-pitched voice again rang in my ears.

Ray Tolbert was a ghost most of the time and a dictator the other few times I was in his presence. I never addressed him as "Dad" or "Father" because I did not acknowledge him. I tried my best not to be in his company for longer than necessary. The aroma that sprouted from his body was overpowering. It reminded me of my mom's clear bottle she drank from before going into work and after getting off, except it also included the fragrance of musty cologne and the smell of a freshly lit cigar. Whenever I saw his thin, lanky frame lounged on our sofa when I got home from school or outside playing with my friends, I quickly vanished to my room. He always sat in the same spot, the right corner of the couch near the door, like he was prepared to leave at any second.

He sat on our sofa, acting like he owned the little apartment we called home, and then grunted every few seconds as if he was trying to clear his throat and show his disapproval at the same time. His burnt crisp charcoal complexion held a tint of gray as if he had never owned a bottle of lotion. His thin lips were just as black as his face, making it hard for me to tell where his mouth began.

Ray was older than my mom and, from his staggering walk, wasn't too far from tumbling into his grave at any moment. The only time he didn't look frail was when he was beating my mom's ass. I wondered where all that strength came from when he looked like a simple cough might burst his lungs. Ray usually never said much to me other than grunting at me and then ordering me to get him a cool drink, except for the time he caught me in my room looking at his playboy magazines. The women's bodies were beautiful, and I was so mesmerized I didn't hear him come into my room.

"Keep yo' lil grimy fangers off my shit!" he yelled, snatching the magazine out of my hands and slapping me across my face with it. "Ya lil boyish ass don't need to look at this."

From that point on, I felt shame every time I was around him. Thankfully, he kept his conversations with me limited, just stared at me, and shook his head. I would have rather kept it that way, therefore, as soon as I saw him, I would disappear into my room until I knew he was gone. Then there were times when I would only hear him without ever seeing him. I would hear him shouting at my mother, knocking her all over the room, and then making his departure while she laid and wept on the floor. The only thing I was grateful for was the simple fact that he did not live with us. I wasn't even sure where he resided, however I was thankful that when he came over, he eventually had to go back to the place he called home.

The stillness of the house was more fearful than what I had ever experienced before and made me wonder if Ray was still here. I slowly opened my closet door and peeped my head out.

After they fought, Ray would leave, and then my mom would come looking for me. I was waiting for her to call my name, but the house was silent.

"This'll be the last time ya put yo' dirty hands on me, Ray Tolbert!" my mom screamed, running past my room. I spotted something in her hand but didn't know what it was until the loudest and most chilling noise filled the whole apartment. Ray's shrieks traveled from the living room to my bedroom and bounced off the walls as another shot erupted from the revolver that my mom possessed.

"You a crazy bitch!" Ray screamed.

"Oh, you ain't seen crazy yet!"

I closed my closet door and pushed myself in the corner again. More tears flowed. "Please, God, protect me," I whispered. I wasn't worried that my mom would hurt me, but I wasn't so sure she wouldn't injure Ray.

•••

Hours passed, and I realized I had cried myself to sleep. The house was quiet now. I stood and opened the closet door to peek outside again.

"Ma," I whispered.

I tiptoed out of the closet as my eyes focused through the darkness.

"Ma," I said again, a little louder.

I stepped out of the bedroom. Once I turned the corner, my scream pushed away the silence. The living room was empty however, splashes of red highlighted the walls, our old tattered tan couch, and the carpet. It looked like someone had dashed red paint all around the living room. Suddenly, the keys jingling in the door snapped me out of my trance. I took off running and locked myself back in my secret place.

I had no idea what was going on. But for now, I knew the only spot I was protected was in my closet. I sobbed until sleep fell upon me.

Chapter 5

Gwen

I sat on my bed, legs dangling off of the side, and waited. The only light in my room was the little ballerina nightlight that was plugged into the wall. The nightlight was a present from my Uncle Bo before he died. The happy thoughts of my Uncle and Rina caused a smile to spread across my face. Even though Uncle Bo was no longer here and couldn't protect me anymore, I always had Rina. I anticipated Rina walking into our room at any second now. After working at the club, she always came home at the same time on Saturday nights. She would come into our bedroom to make sure I was there, and then she would leave to take her bath. After washing up, she would come back into the room and tuck me in. Even though I had already been in bed for hours, she always kissed me on my forehead and told me good night. I could always count on Rina. I would forever depend on my sister.

I heard faint footsteps outside of my bedroom, and my heart stopped pounding. Rina was about fifteen minutes later than usual, but I felt at peace already.

As the door creaked open, I rushed to get under the covers and placed them over my head, so Rina would think I had fallen asleep a while ago. If I wasn't fast asleep, she would question why I was still up this late at night. Instead of her usual voice, I simply heard the same footsteps. I began to think maybe Rina was waiting for me to remove the sheets from over my head until the stench of alcohol and funk invaded the room. The smell was so strong it made me cover my nose with my blanket. The potent odor caused me to cough, and I wondered even more who was in the room with me. I prayed I was dreaming, or this was, in fact, Rina. But that could not have been further from the truth. I peeked from under my sheets and saw him.

Hoping this was just a nightmare, I closed my eyes again. This time, I closed them much tighter and put the sheets back over my head.

"God, please, make him go away. Please, please, make him leave." I silently prayed that when I opened my eyes, he would no longer be in my room. Maybe if I held my breath, I could imagine I was somewhere else, and he would disappear. This had to be a terrible dream. It just had to be.

However, once I heard the click of my bedroom door lock, I knew he wasn't going anywhere. I looked from under the covers, and he was still there. This time, he was closer to my bed. He said nothing as he shuffled toward to me. As if he sensed my next move, his course voice drowned out the silence of the room.

"If ya cry or scream, Imma beat ya," Uncle Lee growled, standing over the bed, daring me to make any kind of noise. His breath reeked of the same foul smell emanating from his body.

"Keep ya mouth shut, or ya gonna be sorry," he threatened.

Uncle Lee snatched the sheets from my legs in one quick movement, exposing my white nightgown that covered my shaking body. His half-washed hands still had spots of oil on them, and red dirt was caked under his fingernails. I wanted to scream and cry, but I remembered his threat and remained silent. I just prayed. Prayed Rina would open the bedroom door at any moment now. I prayed she would save me and never let anyone hurt me like she had promised.

"Take your draws off," Uncle Lee demanded, his eyes searching my body as if he were trying to decide where he wanted to start.

I heard him, but I could not move. Fear had me frozen and pinned to the bed. His voice seemed so far away and close at the same time. Never had I been so scared, so horrified that when I felt the warm urine flowing down my legs, I was not the least bit surprised. Maybe, just maybe, this would deter Uncle Lee from going along with his mission.

Uncle Lee took off his dingy gray T-shirt and threw it on the bed at me. The most menacing laugh left his mouth and struck my ears. "Clean dat piss up and open ya legs, gal."

Again, I was paralyzed. However, this time Uncle Lee didn't stand over me and wait. He snatched his shirt from the bed and wiped the urine from my legs. Then he grabbed the top of my crisp white underwear and snatched on them, ripping them from my body.

Forgetting what I was instructed not to do earlier, a shriek slipped from my lips. As soon as the sound came out of my mouth, it was met with Uncle Lee's fist.

"I told you to hush! Don't make another goddamn sound!"

This time, I did as I was told. My silent tears fell onto my pillow. I turned my head as he unzipped his pants, exposing himself. The unfamiliar pole that emerged from his pants almost caused me to vomit. The pain that followed when he planted himself on top of me and thrust his manhood into my body felt like someone was slicing open my tiny frame and ripping my soul apart. The blood came fast and warm like the pee that had flowed earlier. The snake between his legs entered my shaking body, snatched my innocence, and stole what I had left of my childhood. Inside I screamed for Rina. Where was she, and why had she not come back to save me? Why didn't she rescue me? Why was he doing this to me?

I begged him to stop. I cried and pleaded for him to get up, but that only caused him to cover my mouth and push himself into me harder and faster. "Please, God, let me die. Please, I don't want to live anymore." The only thing I wanted God to do now was to take my life. I would rather be dead than have to undergo any more of this torture. Death would be my release from this agony.

Finally, after what seemed like an eternity, the pounding and pushing stopped. Uncle Lee, sweaty on top of me, groaned as his body shook. His scent strangled me until I feared I would vomit on him like I almost did earlier. Suddenly, he lifted himself off of me and stood beside the bed, yanking his pants up from around his ankles.

"If ya tell, I'll beat ya. I'll beat ya, and no one will believe ya."

I turned on my side and cried into my pillow. I touched the inside of my thigh and noticed I was still bleeding. Blood dripped onto my sheets, causing a sticky mess underneath me, but I did not move.

Lying in the puddle of my own fluids didn't matter to me now. Everything inside of me that was pure had been taken in less than twenty minutes. I was simply what my grandmother always said I was. Same as Ruth Ann, not worth shit. As Uncle Lee had said, beating me to death would be so much better than ever having to go through what just happened or living with the fact that I was now ruined. Not worth shit.

Chapter 6

ClaRina

Mother Clara was never one of those Bible-toting Jesus types knocking down the doors of the church every Sunday. The only time I had ever seen her attend a church service was for one of her brothers' funeral a few years ago. Even though she did not visit the Lord's house, she made sure we went every Sunday. Sunday mornings at seven on the dot, her heavy feet dragged across the worn tan shag carpet of our bedroom.

"Git y'all asses up fo church," she bellowed, suspending my dreams and thrusting me into reality. If we took a minute too long to get out of bed, sure enough, the belt would demand us to rise.

Gwen and I dressed in our Sunday's best, which meant one of the only two dresses that did not have visible holes in them. Once dressed, we walked a mile to my grandmothers' sister's house to ride with her to church. My great-aunt, Marie, was the complete opposite of Mother Clara when it came to her beliefs about church. Her tiny silhouette was nothing more than a proclaimed temple of God. She gossiped about Jesus as if only she was honored enough to know when He was coming back. Every chance she got, she reminded Gwen and me that if we disobeyed His word, we were going straight to hell. I sometimes wondered if I had committed an unforgivable sin in a former life and was already living my days in hell.

This Sunday morning, like every other Sunday morning, we trotted down our dirt road and headed toward Aunt Marie's house. It began to drizzle, making me speed up, so we would not be caught in the upcoming rain.

"Move, slowpoke," I said, gently pushing Gwen in her back. I waited for her to turn around and shove me back or say something smart, but it never came. She was unusually quiet this morning.

"You all right, Gwen? Come on, so we don't git wet," I said, nudging her again.

Gwen's arms were folded across her chest, wrinkling her hand-me-down faded purple flower dress. Head hanging down, she dragged her feet across the dirt and rocks, scratching the soles of my once white Sunday shoes.

"Where were you last night?" Gwen squeaked. She didn't turn around but continued to walk in front of me as we got closer to Aunt Marie's driveway.

"What?" I asked, pausing for a second. "Ya know I was at the club."

"You said you was gonna be in the house right after ya came from the club. Where did ya go?" she demanded. She stopped walking and turned around, finally facing me.

Gwen's right eye was swollen with a dark purple circle around it, and her lip was bruised. Tears trickled down both of her cheeks. "You was supposed to come home."

"Gwen, what happened?" I reached out and grabbed her, allowing her to cry in my arms. I rocked her back and forth. I was rushing so much to get dressed this morning that I had not paid her any attention and didn't even see the bruises.

"He came in the room last night…"

Knowing that one of my worst fears had come true, I placed my hand over Gwen's mouth before she could utter another word.

"Shhh, sis," I said, holding her tighter. I could not bear to hear what I already knew. I could not handle Gwen saying those words to me. The same thing that happened to me happened to her. Her innocence was shattered, and there was nothing I could do. Nothing I could say to take away the pain I knew she was feeling inside.

Tears began to form in the corners of my eyes. "I'll never let anyone hurt you anymore, I promise," I said, stroking my sister's soft curly hair.

From that moment on, I knew I had to protect her no matter what. I would put my life on the line so that no one else could ever harm her again.

•••

School had finally ended for the year, and I was overjoyed. The taunting and lurid abuse were enough to last a lifetime. I fell on my knees night after night and prayed that God would gift me with milky white skin and green or blue eyes so that the attacks would stop. However, every morning, it seemed as if I woke up even darker than the day before.

"Come on, Rina!" Gwen shouted, running past me toward the club. I wandered around outside, shifting through the fields, in and out of cotton stalks, enjoying a little bit of freedom and sunlight before I started on my chores. The high temperatures were excruciating during the summer months in the South, but even the intense humidity could not prevent me from basking in nature today. The heat of hell would have been better than the icy coldness of those four walls of the school building we had just been relinquished from.

Today, we were cleaning up for the Timmonsville Annual Hog Festival. Once a year, all of the black folks in our town migrated to the club on a Saturday morning and partied until late Sunday night. Grandpa Henry would slaughter the thickest, ripest hog and cook it in his pit. The pit was a complete replica of what I imagined hell to be. Looking down into the hole had to be as close as staring into the opening of Satan's playground with shooting flames ascending from the bottomless cavity of doom.

My grandfather would shove a long stick straight through the center of the slop-filled animal. Every few minutes, he turned it around to make sure it was grilled on all sides. The first time I saw him do this, I had nightmares for weeks.

I dreamed three pigs were chasing me, so they could put me on the stick and roast me. As soon as they would get close to catching me, I would always wake up screaming and in tears.

Most nights, I hushed my cries before I woke Mother Clara. But there were other nights that I was not so fortunate, and she would come in and beat me back to sleep.

I strolled the half-mile to the club and contemplated turning around once I saw all the work that had to be done. Beer bottles, pool sticks, and trash were tossed around everywhere as if there had been an explosion the night before. Knowing how the club operated, there was probably a fight or two that caused this disaster. I had been working in the club on the weekends since I was fifteen as a bartender. Every weekend, I could bet there would be some calamity that would lead to the club shutting down earlier than it was supposed to.

Now that I was seventeen, manning the bar was fairly easy. The drinks ordered were simple enough for me to prepare without knowing how alcohol tasted or what mixed well together.

Mostly, clubbers ordered a shot of straight liquor or a mix of liquor and splash of Coke. Then there were the ones requesting just a beer, which allowed me to hand them a can or bottle and focus back on the drunks that littered the dancefloor. Even though many saw my family's club as the wildest place in town to be at night, I detested it. Shoot-outs seemed to occur every weekend, and I had to constantly fight off men from taking advantage of me. Older men, family, and friends were alike, and no one cared if the same blood flowed through our veins when trying to get to a Kendall girl.

"Damn," I mumbled under my breath as I passed my Great-Uncle Lewis, heading to the small stockroom behind the bar.

Great-Uncle Lewis was Mother Clara's baby brother and was seldom sober. If I ever ran into him and he was not intoxicated, he definitely would be in an hour or two.

He never tried to take advantage of Gwen or me, unlike my Uncle Lee, but he was known to have sticky fingers. Mother Clara said he could steal the stank off shit if it were close enough to him. I did not exactly understand what that meant at first until Aunt Flo lost her necklace our mom had sent her for her birthday. The next day, I saw Uncle Lewis with it around his neck, and the saying made complete sense.

Mother Clara had given birth to six children. She had four boys: George, Dale, Bo, and Lee, and two girls, my mom, and Florence. Now there were only five of them. Out of all my uncles, Bo had been the most compassionate one. He was tall like Grandpa Henry but slim and had the most sincere, loving eyes I had ever seen. The type of eyes that let me know I could trust him. He would frequently tell us stories about our mom and let us know she left for us. I didn't comprehend how her leaving helped Gwen and me, but I always listened to whatever Uncle Bo said. And whenever he was not talking about our mother, he simply asked, "Little Rina, you okay? If you not all right, I am here." He used to ask me this at least two or three times a week.

Six years ago, Uncle Bo was killed in a car accident coming from one of his friends' houses. Rumors circulated in our small town that Uncle Bo had made a few of the local white boys angry by taking up for Kathy, a young black girl who lived down the street from us. Mother Clara sent Bo to town for a few groceries, and Kathy was standing outside, surrounded by a group of white guys Bo's age.

Kathy was only thirteen. With Bo being older, he felt the need to help her. He grabbed Kathy and took her into the store with him, ignoring the threats that the guys would make him pay for interrupting the good time they were having and planning. He took Kathy home and told her parents what happened. They were beyond grateful for him protecting their daughter.

Later that night, Uncle Bo was heading home from his friend Chris' house and was said to have lost control of his car. That is what the police told us as well.

However, a witness driving by informed us that she witnessed a red pick-up truck, the same truck that one of the white guys from the store owned, chasing Uncle Bo. They ran him off the road, causing him to crash into a tree. Once word got out about Uncle Bo's accident, Kathy's mother informed Mother Clara of what occurred at the grocery store earlier that day. Grandpa Henry attempted to get justice. But no matter how much power or money one has when one is black, nothing will ever be done to help that person. So, we had to deal with losing Uncle Bo, the one bright light of our family.

When he died, I wept because I knew no one would ever ask if I was okay again.

Uncle George was the eldest of Mother Clara's children. His bald head, almond skin, and short limbs, coupled with the fact he always wore green, made him look like a grumpy meager elf. Uncle George and his wife, Aunt FeFe, lived a street over from Mother's house. Aunt FeFe, whose real name was never mentioned to me, could regularly be found at the club flirting with other men with a cigarette hanging from her lips. Uncle George constantly lied on Gwen and me and was the reason we got fifty percent of our beatings. I could not understand why he received so much pleasure in getting us in trouble or wanted to see us beat so badly. I just attributed it to the fact that he was a callous, miserable old man and had absolutely nothing better to do with his time.

Uncle Dale and Uncle Lee still lived at Mother's house with us. All my uncles worked in the club, but Uncle Dale was the one who managed it alongside my grandfather.

Uncle Dale was known as one of the boldest and toughest men in Timmonsville. He was born with a birth defect that caused one of his legs to be longer than the other.

He walked with a limp and dragged his right foot since that was the one that extended further than the left. His belly expanded so far over his pants that he looked like he was about to give birth to twins at a moment's notice. Even with his deformity and size, that did not stop Uncle Dale from battling anyone who challenged him.

Uncle Dale limped around with his cane and dared anyone to even look at him sideways. On his hip, he always carried an antique revolver that modeled one from an old Western movie. Everyone who knew him or was just familiar with Uncle Dale referred to him as "Nothing but hell" Dale. If any man even attempted to test him, sure enough, it would be his final day walking this earth.

Then there was Uncle Lee, the devil himself. Uncle Lee on the outside, looked harmless, standing at almost six feet with a slender frame. His coffee-colored skin and lean frame posed anything but a threat to those who were unfamiliar with him. However, to me and Gwen he was Satan reincarnated. Evil and nastiness embodied him and rendered him the man that made my skin crawl every time I had to encounter him.

"You gonna clean this up, lil gal?" my Uncle Lewis slurred, pointing at the broken bottles on the floor behind the bar. His eyes were half-closed, and he swayed every time he took a breath. His inability to call me by my name did not surprise me since he never did, but what was shocking was how he remained standing after looking like if he was about to topple over at any minute.

"Yes, sir," I said, scrambling behind him to grab the broom so that I could start sweeping. Out of the corner of my eye, I watched him snatch an opened gin bottle from behind the bar and guzzle it as if it were water quenching his thirst after being out in the fields all day. As I continued to sweep, I daydreamed about when I could leave this place and never return.

●●●

"Ri Ri, wake up." The sudden shaking of my arm caused me to open my eyes and stare into Gwen's face. She was two inches away from me, looking at me with her big brown eyes.

"Gwen? What do you want?" I asked, turning my back to her. It was Friday night, and we had spent all day cleaning. I was weary and just wanted to rest.

"Shhhh…listen to that, Ri Ri! Something's goin' on in Mother's room."

I tried going back to sleep. But now that I was up, I could hear the gruesome sounds that Gwen was referring to.

"Slide over." Gwen pushed me so that she could fit in my bed.

Boom! Boom! The blasts were followed by Mother Clara's screams crowding our tiny room. The sounds wrapped around our beds and felt so close that we instantly put our hands over our ears. I heard Grandpa Henry yelling but could not make out exactly what he was saying. Mother's screams suffocated us as we stared at each other unable to speak.

"I'm scared," Gwen finally whispered, cuddling up to me in bed. "What's going on, Ri Ri? What are they doing in there?"

"Hush up and close your eyes ni." I couldn't tell her that I was frightened, too. These sounds were not like the ones I normally heard at night.

I often heard Grandpa Henry shouting. But this time, it was different. The bass of his voice shook the walls of our room, making my heart pound.

There was one last thump, and the house fell silent. It wasn't a normal silence, though. It was an eerie quiet. The kind of quiet where I knew something was amiss. The kind of quiet that made my heart want to jump out of my chest. The kind of quiet that made Gwen cuddle up next to me even more and bury her head into my bosom.

"Shhhh," I told her as I gently began rocking her to sleep. Something happened. I did not know what, but we would find out soon enough.

Chapter 7

Gwen

I stirred around in Rina's bed, quickly realizing that I was alone. After the events of last night, I had a difficult time going back to sleep. My sister insisted we would be all right. But even with her reassurance, I was still anxious. A part of me wanted to know what all the commotion was, and then, another part just wanted to forget I had heard any of it.

I sat straight up in bed once I heard two unfamiliar voices. I could easily get in trouble for being nosey, so my best bet was to lie back down and pretend I was still sleeping while trying to learn what the two strangers were saying. The men spoke loudly, and I could make out the words "land, to keep things quiet, and prosecute." I didn't know what prosecute meant. But by the way the man stressed the word and reiterated it multiple times, it could not be good.

The unknown men kept talking. My nosiness got the better of me, and I climbed out of bed and tiptoed over to my bedroom door. The floorboards squeaked under my feet, causing me to pause for a second fearful that someone heard I was up. I gently pressed my ear against the wood to hear more of what the men were saying. Words like "cooperate" and "jail" seeped through the closed door. Something was wrong. Just as I pressed myself harder against the door, it swung open. I was face to face with my sister.

"Move!" Rina pushed me out the way and walked toward her bed.

"What's going on?" I asked. Rina had the same look on her face as I did whenever I was fussed at. A mixture of torment and anger.

"Come here, Gwen." Rina sat down and patted the bed, urging me to sit next to her.

"Ri Ri, just tell me what's going on," my voice cracked. Something awful had transpired, and I was terrified for Rina to even tell me what it was.

Rina patted the bed again. "Come on, Gwen," she said in the calm voice she always used to either get me to be silent or stop crying. I had the feeling that whatever it was would make me shed tears real soon.

I slowly dragged my feet across the carpet and walked toward the bed. I plopped down beside my big sister and pulled my gown over my knees. Rina grabbed my hands. "Look at me," she insisted.

I did not want to, but I knew she was going to make me. Tears were already forming, even before she spoke a word.

"Gwen, Grandpa Henry died last night."

As the words registered in my head, I began to cry. "H-h-how?" I managed to ask in between sobs.

"I don't know. Mother says he accidentally fell while they were arguing. That's what she told the police, but they don't believe her."

"Why?" I stared at Rina. "Why don't they believe her? Are the police who I heard talking in there?"

"They think she killed him." Rina's voice was cold now. I wondered why she wasn't crying, too.

"What do you think happened? Do you think the men are right?"

"Shhh, sis, I'm not sho'. But we gotta go stay with Aunt Marie for a few days."

Rina wrapped her arms around me and held me. Even though Grandpa Henry was everything but kind to me, I did not want him to die. I closed my eyes and allowed Rina's arms to provide the comfort they always had.

•••

The two weeks we spent at Aunt Marie's house was equal to being at the pearly gates and having Jesus read out all of our sins one by one. Aunt Marie drilled in our heads that if we did not always do the proper things, we would burn for eternity. By the fifth day, I was more fearful of God than Mother Clara and Grandpa Henry combined.

Rina told me that we were staying here until Mother Clara came back home. Apparently, the blue-uniformed, gun-toting white men who came to question Mother about Grandpa Henry's death had taken her with them. Rina was assured that Mother would be back soon, but I prayed they would keep her. Even though I was now having nightmares of God tossing me into a lake of fire, it was way more bearable than being beat to sleep almost every other night. Living with Aunt Marie was also better than worrying that each footstep I heard by my door was Uncle Lee coming back to make me bleed again. At least when I woke up, I was not sore and was untouched. For that, I endured the chilling stories about burning forever. Mother Clara could stay away for as long as she wanted if the decision were up to me.

After Aunt Marie read about Noah and the big fish to us, I heard Rina enter the room as I nestled in bed.

"Tomorrow, we are going home," Rina said right before she climbed into bed next to me.

Again, I felt defeated and wished that God really was throwing me into the fiery sea that I was sure I would dream about tonight. I would rather burn than go back to that hellish house.

Chapter 8

ClaRina

The trial against Mother Clara was brief and determined that she was defending herself against Grandpa Henry. She was away for almost two weeks, and Grandpa Henry was not buried until Mother Clara returned home. We only heard bits and pieces of what took place from our uncles gossiping with each other. However, even though she was proven innocent, the "white man," as my uncles called him, managed to take away five acres of family land. I was too young to understand how this happened since Mother Clara was not guilty of killing Grandpa Henry, but I just chalked it up to merely being the incorrect color. Being black always seemed wrong.

Ruth Ann came home for the funeral of her father. Even though she was my mother, I never called her "Mom." She was Ruth Ann to me, just like she was to everyone else. She was not special to me, and neither was I to her. She was indeed my mother, yet she was still a stranger in my heart.

I sauntered in the back door of St. Mark's Baptist Church and spotted Ruth Ann walking toward the front of the church. Trailing closely behind her was my baby sister, Beatrice. They looked like New York, and nothing like us. Beatrice wore a yellow polka-dotted dress that flared out from the waist down. Her thick black ponytails stopped at her shoulders, and a look of uncertainty covered her thin, oval copper-colored face. Our eyes met for a few seconds before she looked away. My mom, head held high, was dressed in a simple black form-fitting dress that stopped right above her knees. A grey and black scarf decorated her neck and sunglasses covered her eyes. She glanced in my direction and then turned her head. She stepped towards Grandpa Henry's casket in her patent leather black heels and quickly glanced at him while making her way to her seat.

I looked down at the off-black dress Mother Clara had given me for this occasion. Comparing my mom and sister's outfits to mine confirmed that we indeed were from two different worlds.

In my seventeen years, this was only my second time seeing my mother. Our first introduction that I could remember was when I was eleven. She had come home when Uncle Bo died. As she entered the house after Uncle Bo's funeral, Mother Clara pushed me toward her as if to offer me up as a sacrifice and instructed me to speak to my mother.

I looked this stranger up and down and whispered, "Hello." Then just as quickly, I was pushed into my room and denied access to her again. Now looking at her, she was no more familiar to me than at our first encounter.

I hesitantly walked up to the stone-gray casket, sitting in the front of the church, and peered down at Grandpa Henry. As I looked at him, I felt pure hatred. He was a cold-blooded and insulting man who never spoke any loving or warm words to me. All my life, the only thing he did was bark orders at me. I was never good enough, never strong enough for him. And in-between the ridicule were the nights I tried to forget. The nights I struggled to keep him off me. I stared at him in the casket, and it took everything in me not to hock up a mouthful of saliva and let it loose in the old dead man's face. Between him and Mother Clara, I had no idea how I managed to wake up and still function properly.

After two hours of family and friends telling lies of how much Grandpa Henry would be missed and Rev. Daniels hollering about how Grandpa Henry was a pillar in the community, the funeral was finally over. The repast was held at our house, allowing everyone to gather, eat chicken, and speculate how Grandpa Henry died.

"Gal, go in that kitchen, and git me some water," Mother roared. She had been quiet all day. No tears were shed at the funeral. No sadness or emotions were shown.

She sat still, lifeless, and never once viewed Grandpa Henry in his casket. Dressed in an all-black, two-piece jacket and skirt set, and a faded black church hat, her large body was dead weight on the pew as if she could have been lying beside him.

"Yes, ma'am," I mumbled quickly. I jumped up from the chair I had been sitting in, not wanting to feel the belt today.

I glanced over to the other side of the room and saw Ruth Ann, sitting in the corner on a folded chair, shades covering her eyes as if the sunrays had crept into the house and were beaming directly on her. Her avoidance of me was direct and intentional at the same time.

Entering the kitchen, I passed Uncle Dale leaning on his cane and telling Uncle Lee that the club would open in a few hours to celebrate Grandpa's life. I rolled my eyes and headed to the refrigerator to retrieve the bottle of water.

"Rina, you gonna work tonight," Uncle Dale said, without looking at me.

"Yes, sir," I replied, even though I knew he was not really asking me. I wanted to scream hell no; instead, I just poured the water into a glass and walked out of the kitchen.

I said a little prayer that tonight would not end in gunshots. Then I sent up another prayer asking God to at least pay attention to one of my pleas. I felt like whenever I prayed, God was napping since He never seemed to hear me. Maybe, just maybe, tonight, God would be awake and listen.

•••

I was behind the bar fixing a gin and orange juice for Mr. Joe Rollins, who practically lived at the club. Every time the doors opened, best believe, Mr. Joe would be one of the first to enter.

"Ya lookin' good in dem britches, Rina," he slurred, referencing my white bell-bottom pants. His red clay-colored, dusty hands reached into his overall jeans pockets, pulled out a five-dollar bill, and handed it to me. I reached for the money and noticed the caked-up dirt under his long yellow fingernails. He held my hand two seconds too long as his beady bloodshot eyes roamed up and down my body, making me want to vomit.

I snatched my hand back, slid the drink over to him, and moved to the far end of the bar. This was the kind of stuff I dealt with every night I worked at the club. Old men making passes at me, and most of them were my own family.

Mother Clara stood behind me in the kitchen, frying chicken and making plates for the club goers. My mouth watered at the sweet aroma floating past me and beckoning to everyone crowded around on the walls and dancefloor to get a taste. Mr. Joe smiled at me, revealing his brown stained teeth, tilted his ragged navy-blue hat, and slowly hopped off the barstool he had been perched on top of for the past hour. Praying he would not come over to where I was standing, he began to hobble toward me.

Another unanswered prayer, I thought, glancing toward the ceiling and rolling my eyes. As if the Lord was checking in on me at that very moment, Mr. Joe slid right past me into the kitchen where Mother Clara was.

For the first time, I felt that God had taken a little pity on me. I didn't know how long His mercy would last. But as of right now, I was overwhelmingly grateful.

However, I didn't get to revel in the moment for long. As I was fixing a drink for Mrs. Linda, another constant at the club, I heard Mother Clara scream out a string of curse words.

"Muthafucka, ya gonna die tonight!" Mother Clara shouted.

Instantly, I turned around to see what was going on. Mother Clara had Mr. Joe pinned up against the refrigerator with her pearl handle twenty-two pistol pressed against his temple.

"Please, Clara, please just lemme go! I ain't mean no harm," Mr. Joe whimpered, begging for his life. Mother pressed the gun harder into the side of his head.

As if he was watching the entire time, Uncle Lee ran across the club from the dancefloor toward the kitchen.

Right before he could get there, Mother dropped her gun, closed both of her hands around Mr. Joe's neck, and threw him out of the kitchen and across the bar as if he was a mere five-pound potato sack. As if this was not enough, another fight ensued on the opposite side of the club at that moment near the door.

"I'll kill 'er one of ya bastards!" Uncle Dale screamed.

My eyes had been so focused on Mr. Joe's still body lying in front of the bar that I almost missed the action near the entrance. I glanced up and saw Uncle Dale pointing a twelve-gauge shotgun where the fighting was taking place.

Pop! Pop!

A shot rang out from behind Uncle Dale's head before he had a chance to fire his weapon. Among the screams and people running to get out of the club, another shot rang out. Before I could fall to the floor for cover, I saw Uncle Dale grab his good leg as blood gushed from it.

"Call the ambulance; call the doctor!" Uncle Lee screamed, running from the kitchen, holding a bottle of gin in his hand.

As Uncle Dale held on to his wounded leg, blood oozed through his hand; he grabbed the shotgun that had landed on the floor beside him. He pointed at the location where the previous shots had come from and blasted five rounds with his free hand.

People were still scrambling, trying to vacate the club. From past experiences, I learned to stay close to the floor in one spot until it was safe for me to get up. Uncle Dale fired one more shot right before the ambulance came to put him on the gurney and haul him away. The entire time he was on the stretcher, he was cursing and promising he would kill whoever had shot him.

Once they took him outside, silence descended upon the club. I slowly got up and saw Mother Clara standing at the entrance.

"Gal, git on to the safe box and start countin' down that money," Mother ordered as soon she caught a glimpse of me. "Make sure it's all there 'fore we go to the hospital."

"Yes, ma'am," I responded, scurrying to the small room in the back where the money was kept.

Uncle Dale may have just gotten shot, but nothing was more important in my family's eyes than making sure the money was accounted for and safe. I said another quick prayer and asked God to make sure Uncle Dale survived. The way my prayers went unanswered, I was sure this would be one He ignored, too, which was exactly what I wanted.

Chapter 9

Beatrice

"Y'all soooo country!" I turned my nose up at Gwen, who had red mud smeared on the top part of her already dirty blue jean overalls. There was no way my mother would have allowed me to be seen like that. I stood from my seat on the porch and smoothed out the wrinkles of my pink frilly summer dress. The matching bows dangling from my hair was a bit much, but I knew why my mom had me all dressed up just to play outside. Even though we struggled and barely had enough to eat in New York, my mom made sure no one ever knew we lacked anything, especially when we traveled down here to the South to visit a family I barely knew. The public façade she presented that we were doing beyond well in the big city of New York—she and I knew it was the farthest thing from the truth.

On the ride down, Ruth Ann turned to me and said, "Bea, look at me and listen to what I say." My mom was serious whenever she demanded my full attention, so I stared straight at her and did not try to interrupt what she was about to tell me.

"Don't go down here and tell dese folks anything. They family, but that is it. They don't need to know our business. Hear me, and hear me good, girl."

I nodded, "Yes, ma'am." I didn't dare ask why we had to be so secretive while we were down here. I was just going to do what my mom asked in hopes that being here would be better than hiding in my closet.

We were only here for two days just so my mom could "make sure the old man was dead," as she put it. I had met Grandpa Henry once when we visited for a funeral a few years ago, and that single time was enough for me.

He did not acknowledge my mother nor me, and whenever he walked into the room, my mother made us get up and leave. I feared him and had no idea why, other than he looked terrifying.

The funeral was yesterday, and I was ready to go back home. The only good thing about being here was the food. I had not felt my normal hunger pains since we had arrived.

"Ya don't belong here no way," Chris said, running past me. Chris was the son of one of my uncles I didn't know. As a matter of fact, I wasn't familiar with any of my cousins, and I didn't want to be. I barely knew my own sisters. But one thing I learned from practically raising myself was that no one was going to punk me. I was not going to allow anyone to talk to me like I could not be here.

I walked up to Chris, stood directly in front of him, gathered some spit in my mouth, and let him have it right in his face. I balled up my fists, expecting Chris to come charging at me; instead, he let out a loud cry and ran toward the house.

"Beatrice!" Rina shouted, marching toward me. "I can't believe ya did dat!" Little did I know she had been observing the entire thing only a few feet away from us.

"He started it!" I rolled my eyes at my sister. She was older than me, but I was not going to let her talk down to me, either. I was an outsider and had to protect myself from these country bamas.

Rina reached out her hand, asking me to take it. I took a few steps back to widen the distance between us.

"It's okay, Bea, you can trust me," she said as if she could read my mind. I stared at her, and for some reason, it felt like I could honestly believe her, a feeling I had never experienced before.

I took two steps toward my sister and grabbed her hand.

She didn't look any better than Gwen in her faded black jeans and white stained T-shirt, but the fact that she was attempting to protect me meant something to me. As soon as my hand was in hers, another one of my unknown cousins, Eve, Chris's sister, came rushing toward us.

"So just 'cause ya from the big city, ya think ya can spit in folks' face, huh?" she screamed. Before she could get directly in front of me, Rina stood between us, blocking her sight of me.

"Eve, it was just a lil disagreement. Everybody's okay."

"Rina, I know that's ya lil sister, but somebody needs to tear her ass up."

"Well, you ain't…" I started saying while trying to push Rina to the side so that I could face Eve.

Rina glanced back at me. "I got this," she whispered.

"Ni, Eve, ya know Bea ain't mean no harm. But I'll go and have a good talkin' to her." Rina grabbed my hand again, tighter this time. She pulled me away before Eve could respond.

Behind us, I could still hear Eve fussing. Rina continued to pull me until we were far away on the other side of Grandpa's yard. Not knowing what Rina was going to do to me, I prepared myself to fight her as well. I was small, but I feared no one.

As soon as we stopped, I snatched my hand away from her. Rina turned around, looked at me, and smiled. "Baby sis, I know ya don't know me, but we blood. You my little sister, and I'll always be here for you."

I didn't know whether to believe her or not, but I really wanted to. No one had ever talked to me so kind and gentle like this before.

Then, to my surprise, my older sister reached out and put her arms around me. She gave me a long, tight embrace. For the first time in my life, I felt like someone cared for me.

I didn't exactly know what this feeling was. But from what I had heard and seen on TV; it must have been love.

•••

"Bitch, you still ain't no good. Just 'cause you moved from here, don't mean shit. You ain't shit and won't ever be shit!"

I was awakened by loud voices. After having another scrumptious meal of fried chicken, turnip greens, rice, gravy, and sweet cornbread, I was knocked out in the bed with Rina.

I was sleeping so peacefully I had forgotten where I was. For the first time, I slept without having any nightmares of being chased or hiding out. Tonight, my dreams were of my upcoming eleventh birthday. I was sitting in a huge area surrounded by presents. The room was filled with balloons and a beautiful pink princess cake. As I was about to cut into my cake, I was suddenly awakened by my mom's screams.

"I'm glad the old man's dead! I hated him, and I hate y'all, even mo'!"

I jumped up and automatically started to run to my hiding place, thinking that I was in my own room. Before I could get out of bed, Rina grabbed me and placed her hand over my mouth.

"Shhh, Bea," she whispered in my ear. "Everything's gonna be all right. I'm right here."

Rina's words began to calm me, and I started to feel safe again. A few minutes passed, and I was almost drifting back to sleep when the bedroom door swung open. My mom came running in. Her once curled hair was wildly standing on her head, and her red and black-striped shirt was torn.

"Bea, get yo' ass up! We leavin' these crazy folks ret now!" My mom snatched me out of Rina's arms and dragged me from the room and down the hallway.

As we passed by the kitchen to the front door, I saw Uncle Dale charging in from the back. "Yea, git on! Yo' ass ain't welcome here no mo'! Next time I'll kill ya!" Uncle Dale screamed.

My mom rushed me out of the house and over to our car. She opened the car door and slung me inside.

Pop! Pop!

Popping sounds rang in my ears as my mom cranked up the car and threw the gear shift into drive. I knew what that recognizable sound was, so I ducked down, not knowing which way the shots were coming from.

"Y'all some no good muthafuckas! Family ain't shit! I told the fuckin' truth!" my mom screamed out the window as we headed toward the main highway.

"Don't you ever trust those people, Bea! You hear me? Family or not, those some evil nasty bastards, and they are not to be trusted. You hear me?"

"Yes, ma'am," I mumbled.

My mom took her eyes off the road and put them on me to make sure I understood her request. Her eyes were bloodshot and puffy as if she had been crying for hours.

"I mean it, gal. Those people ain't no good, and we don't need 'em. Don't trust 'em and don't ever come down here no mo'! No mo'!"

"Yes, ma'am," I repeated with tears crawling down my cheeks. That would be my last visit to Mother Clara's house to see my sisters, and the only time I ever felt any kind of genuine love.

Chapter 10

Gwen

1966

He was a cool sip of sugar water after working in the fields all day. He was sweeter than the pound cake and syrup biscuits Rina snuck to me after each beating I endured. My melancholy days were pleasingly interrupted by his presence. He made me feel like there was goodness in the world, and one day things would be normal, whatever normal was. He was a gentle hug whenever I wanted to break down and cry, and a simple smile after being told I was nothing. He was my happy.

William Dillard, or Billy, as we called him, lived on the next street over from our house. He was a few years younger than my uncles, just barely tiptoeing into his twenties but could frequently be seen hanging out with them at the club or just around the house.

"How ya doin', pretty girl?" The words danced from his lips and made my private areas heated in the most intensive way.

My fifteen-year-old eyes were fascinated by Billy's lean stature, honey complexion, and curly hair. His eyes were a captivating gray as if they held the secrets of our budding crush.

Now that I was old enough to work in the club, Rina and I rotated between who would bartend and who would stay home to clean up and make sure the house was to Mother Clara's liking. Even though it hardly ever was tidy enough to avoid her punches, I relished the nights where I could be at home alone. Alone without having to look over my shoulder or fear that someone would take advantage of me. However, I had no idea that this night would change my moments of happiness into pure bliss.

I was sweeping the torn carpet in the living room and listening to the old box radio that sat perched upon our wobbly coffee table. The lyrics of "Son of A Preacher Man" filled up the room as I thought about my Billy. Ironically, his dad was a preacher hence why this song was so fitting. I swayed my hips to the beat of the song and stopped suddenly as I heard a soft knock on the front door. The music from the club and my radio usually drowned out my thoughts and the ability to even hear, so I was surprised when I heard the faint banging on the door.

"Who is it?" I asked, wondering who would be bold enough to come to our house when everyone knew all members of the Kendall family were more than likely at the club.

After I didn't get an answer the first time, I asked again. A part of me was nervous to answer the door for apprehension of who may be standing on the opposite side.

"Who is it?" I asked again, trying not to sound worried.

"Billy."

At first, I thought maybe I was just hearing things, but I did not want to ignore the fact that Billy may have really been at the door.

I rushed to open it, and sure enough, the man standing on the other side made my entire body shiver. There stood the guy who secured his way into my dreams nightly and frequented my thoughts daily.

My perfect angel graced my doorway, dressed in a black-shirt and blue jeans, with a huge grin on his gorgeous face. The contagiousness of Billy's smile made one settle on my face as well. I was speechless.

"Wanna go for a walk, pretty girl?"

Billy and I had never been alone together, and his invitation made me uneasy. I would often see him at the club, and we exchanged greetings and smiles. Every so often, I could linger back long enough for him to touch my hand while walking by. Our conversations included him asking me how I was doing and nothing more than that. It was clear that our fondness for each other was mutual. However, never did I think there would come a time where it could just be him and me without anyone else around.

After a few seconds without uttering a word, I reached for Billy's hand and allowed him to lead me out the door.

We walked quietly down the trail off of Springfield Road, which was the road that connected my street to where Billy lived. Once we crossed over to Patterson Road, where Billy's house was, he finally broke his silence.

"Gwen, you trust me?" he asked, glancing at me.

"I do," I mumbled.

"Wanna go to my house? Nobody there."

Even though I knew it was wrong and would more than likely get me into a world of trouble for even being with Billy, I did not want to leave him. Mother Clara made it clear to me and Rina that any mingling with the opposite sex would not be tolerated. She reminded us that we would be a complete reflection of our mother if we had any dealings with boys. However, being in Billy's presence now would be well worth the beating that would follow if she was to ever find out.

"Yeah," I whispered, avoiding Billy's eyes.

"Don't be scared. I ain't gone hurt you."

And for some strange reason, I believed him. The delight I felt with Billy could not be described or even explained. All I knew was that I did not want it to end anytime soon. I deserved just a little bit of happiness with all the misery I had to go through.

•••

"Am I hurting you?" Billy's gray eyes met my brown ones and were filled with concern.

Even though I wasn't a virgin, this feeling was opposite of when Uncle Lee came into my room to grope and grind on top of me.

Shame and humiliation didn't lay beside me and nestle with me until I cried myself to sleep like it did every time my legs were gaped open, and my purity was stripped from me.

Billy was the only boy who had ever kissed me. His gentle kisses found my mouth and moved down my neck. I squirmed as he continued to kiss me and unbutton my shirt. The sudden wetness between my legs was something else I had never felt before. I was certain I hadn't peed on myself, but the moisture I was now experiencing was new to me.

"Billy, do you love me?" I asked. His hands traveled to the button on my jeans. At that moment, I was not sure I knew what being in love looked or felt like. But it had to be this sensation that my heart wanted to leap out of my chest right now.

He stopped suddenly and sat up. We were in his room, lying on his twin bed. Worried that I had ruined the moment, I sat up beside him and began putting my shirt back on.

"I...I—" I began.

"Gwen, you the prettiest girl I ever seen, and yes, I love you. I...I loved you since I first seen ya." Billy's eyes searched his room as if he had misplaced something. He stared at the poster of Marvin Gaye on his blue painted bedroom wall. I grabbed his hand, and he finally looked at me.

He gently kissed me again. "I love you, Gwen," he said once more.

I laid back down on his bed inviting him to continue what we had started.

His lips found mine once again. He kissed my neck, my breasts and finally positioned his naked body on top of mine. He slowly entered me, making sure not to be too rough or hurt me. I exhaled and let go. His entrance into me was effortless; my body surrendered to him. I allowed him to do whatever he wanted, and pleasure overwhelmed my young body. I felt something I had never felt before. I felt wanted, desired, and loved. I prayed and hoped this feeling would last forever.

Chapter 11

Beatrice

"Ain't nothin' but a little mary jane, Bea," my best friend, Sheila, taunted me. The smell reminded me of when Ray came back to visit after being gone for about a week or two. He would walk in reeking of the substance that was in the white thin rolled paper that Sheila was now waving in front of me. Whenever I smelled that stench, it meant he had returned, and the fighting would soon begin again. However, ever since the blood on the walls, I had not seen Ray. I knew better than to inquire about it, but I often wondered what exactly happened to him. All I knew was Mom had taken the gun over to Ms. Ann, our next-door neighbor's house. When the police arrived, they didn't have a weapon or anything to use against her. She told me that I didn't see anything or know anything; therefore, I knew better than to ask questions. It did not appear that he would be coming back. For that, I was beyond glad.

"Give it here den," I snatched the joint from Shelia and put it to my lips.

"Ni just slowly breathe in and blow out," she instructed.

I attempted to do as I was told. But as soon as I blew the smoke out, a trail of coughs followed. I leaned over and tried to catch my breath, but it felt like I was choking on air.

I handed the joint back to Shelia, begging her to take it.

"Ya just pulled too hard," she said matter-of-factly, not concerned that I was about to die.

Still coughing, I managed to stand up straight. I watched as Sheila took a few puffs off the joint as if it was second nature. Finally, I stopped coughing and caught my breath.

She handed the joint back to me, "Dis time, don't pull so hard."

I took the joint once again and gently pulled on it. Unlike before, I was able to blow the smoke out without choking to death.

I had never been the type of girl to smoke or drink since I had seen it so much growing up. My mother lived by her favorite bottle of gin, and as a child, made me promise not to touch her magic juice that she took a swig of every morning before going to work and every night after getting off. The way the clear liquid made her act afterward was the main reason I stayed away from it. Her incapability to form complete sentences, or even to walk straight, was enough for me to wonder why anyone would want to take something that made them look and seem so foolish. However, every single day, she turned the bottle up like it was what she had longed for more than anything else.

"Don't just hold on to it," Sheila demanded, once she noticed I was daydreaming.

We were standing in the alley around the back of my apartment building, where no one could accidentally run into us.

Sheila lived in the same building as me and had been my best friend since we were eight. Now that we were twelve, our bond was unbreakable. I considered her more as a sister than a friend. I felt a closeness with her that I did not have with anyone else. Sheila knew my dreams, my disappointments, and my fears. She never judged me and was always there, more than Ruth Ann and Ray combined. Truth be told, she was my only friend. Sheila's large oval-shaped brown eyes and curvy frame made her one of the prettiest girls in our complex. I was grateful just to be connected with someone so beautiful. I was rather tomboyish and on the slender side. Sheila's silky black tresses made my unkempt afro an embarrassment. However, I admired Shelia's beauty. All the neighborhood girls wanted to be like her, and I was honored that she was my friend.

"My mom cooked pork chops, cabbage, and rice today. You comin' to eat with us?"

I took the joint out of Sheila's hand and took another slow drag.

"Yep," I said, handing it back to her. "I gotta go home and clean up, and I'll be ret down."

"Okay, girl," Sheila replied, taking a few more puffs before putting the joint out and throwing it behind the dumpster. She turned to leave, and I stared at her full hips as she walked away. Every time I was around Sheila, I felt at peace and loved her more.

Dismissing my constant thoughts of my best friend, I focused on getting back home and doing my chores so that I could be in Shelia's presence again. I ran around the back toward my apartment and opened the door. As soon as I walked in, I saw my mom sitting at the kitchen table. Usually, my mom didn't get in until around midnight or later, and I was already in bed.

"Hey, Ma," I said nervously, shocked that she was home and hoping she didn't smell the marijuana I had smoked.

"Bea, come sit down with me for a minute."

"Yes, ma'am," I replied, walking toward the table.

Mom's favorite happy juice was sitting in the middle of the table, next to a small glass that was filled to the brim.

"Bea, I am dying." Her face was without emotions, and she said it like she was simply telling me something as unimportant as the day of the week. Tears immediately began to make their way to the corners of my eyes.

"No tears," she said, once she noticed I was about to cry.

"I got cancer, and the doctor is not sure how long I'll be here. I'm gonna go through this here treatment. But at this point, it's a long shot."

"But, Mom—" I started.

"Hush up, and listen," my mom interrupted before I could utter another word.

"If I die tomorrow, or a year from now, there's a few things I need ya to know and also do for me."

I listened attentively, trying my best to hold my emotions back. As my mom began talking about her pending death, all I could think about was what would happen to me. Who would I live with? Would I have to go down South with my sisters? Would Ray come back and take me with him?

"I have written out everything I need you to do when I die," she continued, handing me a piece of paper.

I grabbed the paper out of her hand but remained quiet.

"Always remember the things I taught you. Never trust anyone. People will always let you down, even family. Hell, especially family. Don't ever let people get too close. They'll always disappoint you."

I continued to listen to my mom repeat the things she constantly told me. I could recite word for word everything she was saying.

And as if she could read my mind, she answered my question without me having to ask. "No, you don't have to move down South when I pass. Ms. Ann is willing to take you in so that you can stay here."

I let out a sigh of relief as if a ten-pound weight had been lifted off me. Even though Ms. Ann was a lot older than my mother, I was already used to her checking in on me from time to time when she knew I was home alone. She didn't do that a lot but often enough.

"Those folks down South may have the same blood as you. But believe me, those bastards ain't yo' kinfolk," Mom said, referencing our family.

"Maybe you won't die," I whispered, finally getting enough courage to say something.

"Bea, if I haven't taught you nothing else, I taught you to be strong and take care of yourself. Everybody gotta die. Do me proud and remember the things I told you."

"Yes, ma'am," I whispered, still confused. No one close to me had ever died before. The only funerals I had been to were the two down South for Uncle Bo and Grandpa Henry. I never knew them, so it really didn't affect me.

My mother took both of my hands in hers. We sat across from each other at the table, just silently staring at one another. This time, when tears slowly rolled down both of my cheeks, she didn't tell me to stop crying. She just looked at me and squeezed my hands tighter. No more words were passed between us as we sat at our dining room table. It was just us. And at that moment, for the first time, I felt love from my mom. The only love I would hold on to way after she was gone.

•••

It was a cold November morning when I buried my mother. There was a light mist in the air, and shades of gray covered the sky. The weather reflected my mood, dismal, and dreary. She was gone from me eight months from the day that we sat down at our kitchen table and shared with me that she was dying. During those few months, I watched my mother wither away and become more of a recluse than she was before. However, I did everything she told me to do and knew she would be proud of me for taking care of her wishes. The only thing I regretted doing was burying her alone. Except for Ms. Ann, who helped me get her arrangements in order, my mother wanted no one there at her graveside burial, and she didn't even want anyone to know about her passing. A part of me thought at least ClaRina and Gwen should have known.

But as far as I could remember, Mother never talked to them, and they didn't call her. So, I kept her death and burial a secret and did what I was told to do.

After the burial, I went back to our apartment to pack alone. Many nights, I had wished I didn't have to hear the fighting or my mom's screaming or see her lying on the floor. Many days I just wanted to get away and be by myself. Often times, I cried myself to sleep in my hiding place, scared to come out. Yet, tonight, things were different. I would have given anything to have my mom cooking breakfast like she used to. But instead, I was lonely. I thought about my mother's words and realized this feeling was what I would have to get used to for the rest of my life.

Chapter 12

Gwen

I lifted my head from the toilet for the third time and gazed at the ceiling. I had been in the bathroom for at least an hour, and I was sure Mother Clara had to be searching for me by now. But as much as I did not want to get in trouble, I couldn't get off the floor. My white blouse was drenched with sweat, and I had made a mess all over it. My stomach flipped over, sending my head right back in the toilet. After vomiting once more, I managed to lift myself and stand this time. If I could only make it to the couch to lie down, at least I wouldn't have to chance Mother Clara finding me in the bathroom throwing up.

Opening the door, I peeked out to see if anyone was coming down the hall. The coast was clear. I walked as fast as I could to the couch and flopped down before the entire room started to spin. I closed my eyes and waited for the feeling to pass.

"Gal, where ya at?" I heard Mother Clara yelling as she entered the kitchen.

I tried to answer, but no words would come out. "Lord, please, let me say something," I silently begged. But as the room continued to rotate, I still could not make a sound.

"Gal, don't make me call ya again," Mother Clara shouted again from the kitchen.

I tried to get up, but my legs wouldn't cooperate at all. At this point, I could not even move.

I closed my eyes. As soon as I did, a ferocious pain traveled up from my leg to my lower back. I screamed, finally able to conjure up a noise. Another pain ripped through my side from right to left. Mother Clara stood over me, ready to unleash another round of vicious strikes upon me.

"Don't ya ever ignore me when I tell ya to come here," she ordered as she tore into my flesh with her belt once again.

Between my earlier sickness and the incredible pain being thrust upon me, I felt like death was soon to follow.

As much as I wanted to tell Mother I was ill, still, no words would come out. I endured the lashings until I was to the point of passing out. The image of Mother standing over me was just a blur as I tried to stay conscious. Unfortunately, my attempts failed as the last blow made me drift off to sleep.

•••

I had been sick off and on for eight weeks now and did my best to hide it from Mother Clara. From what I could tell, I was successful.

ClaRina left for college three months ago, and I wanted my sister more than anything now. I needed her help before Mother Clara figured out what was wrong with me.

"Rina, you coming home today?" I asked, praying her answer would be yes.

"I'll be home tomorrow morning, Gwen. Everything okay?

"I just wanna talk to you. You told me you would be home today," I whined. I was disappointed that Rina had not stuck to her original plans. I had no idea what to do about my problem, and Rina was the only one I knew who could fix it for me. I have always counted on my sister. This time, she had to come through for me. I had no one else to go to.

"Okay, I will be home soon. Whatever you need, ya know I gotcha. I just had to take care of some stuff for one of my classes. But I promise I'll be home tomorrow."

I hung up the phone, and a tremendous fear came over me. I was afraid Rina would not be able to remedy this situation. At this point, I wasn't sure anyone would be able to help.

As soon as I was about to call Rina again to find out the exact time she would be home, Mother Clara walked into my room. Usually, I could hear her feet dragging against the carpet and prepare myself for her arrival. But this time, I guess my mind was so preoccupied that she was able to sneak up on me.

She entered the room and stared down at me in disgust and revulsion like I was fresh roadkill next to one of her beloved cotton stalks.

"Get your fast tail up and come with me," she ordered.

I knew better than to hesitate or ask questions. I did what she told me and followed her out of my room and down the hallway. Thinking she was just going to make me do a chore, I was surprised when she grabbed her jacket, led me outside, and told me to get in the car.

Climbing into the back seat of Mother Clara's brown Monte Carlo, I quietly sat while we proceeded out of our driveway and onto the main road toward town. Even though I knew it was impossible to do, I felt hiding in the back of the car would somehow protect me from Mother Clara. I had no idea where we were going and too scared to inquire about our destination. The only thing I could think of was if Rina had come home like she was supposed to, I wouldn't have been going wherever Mother Clara was taking me.

We rode in silence for ten minutes. Mother didn't turn on the radio or even scold me for what I did wrong. She simply rolled the window halfway down and kept her eyes focused on the road. All I saw the entire ride was the back of her head decorated with her tight greasy jet-black curls. After another five minutes, we pulled off the main highway onto a dirt road.

Mother Clara, still silent, directed the car down the dirt road, which was at least a mile long. My anxiety mixed with nausea almost made me throw up the lunch I had earlier.

I wiped the sweat from my forehead and took long deep breaths to calm myself. Again, I didn't want Mother to get suspicious before I had a chance to talk to Rina and figure out what I would do.

We finally came upon a small redwood house that resembled a cabin in the middle of the woods. There were no cars in the driveway, and the house looked like it had been abandoned years ago.

My curiosity was getting the best of me. I wanted to ask who lived here, and why did we come to their house, but fear held my mouth closed. Mother opened her door and stepped out of the car. As I reached for the handle to get out, she opened it for me and pulled me out of the car.

"Ya think I didn't know?" she asked, dragging me by my shirt to the front door of this unknown house. "Ya think I'm dumb, and I didn't know whatcha been doing?"

I wasn't sure if she wanted me to answer or not, but I prayed she didn't know what I had been trying to hide from her for weeks.

Mother Clara did not wait for me to speak before continuing. "Your fast ass just like your damn mammie. Just like her ass, and I be damned if I take care of yo' kids, too. All you want to do is open yo' legs! That's all ya good fo!"

The tears were now flowing down my face. All I could think about was if Rina were here, then she would have been able to save me. I knew it was wrong, but I was carrying a piece of Billy inside me, and I did not want to let it go. It wasn't made in shame or disgrace; it was made out of love. It was the only good part of me, and I wanted to keep it more than I wanted my own life.

"Please, Mother Clara, please," I pleaded, hoping she would listen to me for once. Wishing she would allow me to keep the one thing about me that was pure. The one thing that wasn't tainted and dirty.

She ignored my cries and continued dragging me to the front door. Mother knocked on the door twice. A voice inside responded that she was coming. My shirt was now torn, exposing my slightly protruding belly.

When the door swung open, my tears subsided. I came face to face with what would be my baby's grim reaper. She stood in the doorway, six feet tall, and blue-black. Her hair looked like a possum had made a home on top of her head and died, thick, unkempt, and in all directions. She looked at me in total and utter hatred, the same way Mother Clara was.

"Thank you, Ms. Alberta, for getting us in so soon," Mother Clara said, pushing me into the house.

Ms. Alberta nodded and led us into her back room. "Sit up there, child," she pointed at the silver table that was in front of me.

I hesitated too long, forcing Mother Clara to push me toward the table. "Get on the damn table, now!" Mother Clara ordered.

I did as I was told, holding back my tears. At this point, I knew there was nothing else that could be said or done.

As I climbed on the cold hard table and spread my legs apart, my quiet tears gained a voice, and I wept. Ms. Alberta handed me a pill to help with the pain. The medicine may have assisted with the discomfort, but the hurt in my heart would never go away. Mother Clara was taking away the only thing that could provide me love. The only part of me that was worthy of love.

I cried while this woman, this stranger, grabbed an instrument that resembled a metal clothes hanger and stuck it inside me. She stirred the tool around, then yanked it out, which followed with a gush of blood.

I held onto the sides of the table as my tears grew louder.

"You did this to yourself," Mother Clara stated. "Now hush up all that damn crying. That'll teach ya to close yo' legs from now on. Just like yo damn mammie."

I turned my head and let the tears fall freely. I was all bad once again. The best part of me had been stricken from me, and there was absolutely nothing I could do about it. Rina wasn't here to save me like she had promised, and now I wasn't worth shit again. And for as long as I lived, I would never forgive Mother Clara for taking away the only joy I had ever had.

Chapter 13

ClaRina

"Ya can't git away from me!" he growled with that familiar sinister expression. "Lil gal, you can never leave me!" As he started to come toward me, I braced myself. Right before, his hefty frame was towering over me, I awakened and sat straight up in my bed. I surveyed the room, slowly realizing that I was still in my dorm. My entire body was shaking and sweat covered my face. *Calm down, Rina. It was just another nightmare.* Although he was now six feet in the ground, he haunted my waking hours and sleep.

The last semester of my junior year was swiftly coming to an end, and the idea of going back to Timmonsville for the summer smothered me. It occupied my mind, making it impossible to concentrate in my classes. I was maintaining a 3.5 GPA in school, but the thought of going home was quickly lowering my good grades.

"You all right, girl?" Rosalyn, my roommate, asked as she entered our dorm room. "You look like you just saw a ghost."

"It was another bad dream," I said, shaking my head. I kicked my covers off me and attempted to erase the dream from my mind.

Rosalyn sat on her bed directly across from mine and stared at me as if I was a problem on her exam she couldn't quite comprehend. "Rina, you wake up every night screaming like someone is trying to kill you. That's not good, girl."

"I know. I know." I sighed. "I will get it together soon."

"I hope so. I don't wanna see you failing classes because of this," Rosalyn said in her most motherly tone. She pulled her medium-length black hair back into a ponytail and stared at me for a few seconds more.

"I promise I will be okay," I repeated, trying to convince her. I stared at her as jealousy swept over me. Roselyn was not only an extremely beautiful girl with a slim model figure, sandy complexion, and alluring wide eyes, but she also came from a loving, close-knit family. Her parents had been married for thirty-four years and called her three times a week just to tell her how proud they were of her and how much they loved her. I could only fantasize about having someone in my family constantly reminding me of how much I was loved.

Finally, she gathered her denim jacket lying across her bed and headed toward the door. Before exiting, she turned back around and stared at me again. "Rina, we gonna talk more about this when I get back from class." She closed the door behind her, and again, my mind went back to this summer.

Rosalyn was right; me missing sleep and making myself ill about going back home was not healthy. I needed to come up with a plan so I would not have to go back to the pits of hell this summer. I glanced at the picture of Harold and me hanging on my mirror, and a smile instantly replaced the frustration that had been plastered on my face since I had awakened from my nap.

My dear, Harold. We had been dating since my freshman year, and I knew he loved me. He graduated last year and took a job in Atlanta, Georgia. Even though we were three hours away from each other now, Harold still went to great lengths to show me that he still cared deeply for me. We talked on the phone daily, and he came home every weekend to be with me. We even talked about getting married once I graduated college in a year. Before I could pick up the phone to call Harold, it began to ring.

"Hello," I cleared my voice so the other person on the line wouldn't be able to tell I had just woken up not too long ago. Gwen and Harold were the only two people who constantly called me. Both knew my schedule and that I was supposed to be in class right now. However, I was more tired during the day because of the recent nightmares, and I had started missing classes here and there to get some rest.

"Hey, baby," Harold's baritone voice made me smile even wider than before when I glanced at our picture. As soon as I heard his soothing greeting, I knew what I had to do.

"Hey, Harold," I said tenderly.

"Baby, what's wrong, and why are you not in class?"

"Harold, do you love me?" I asked.

"Of course, I do, Rina. Is something wrong?" he questioned.

"Marry me, Harold."

"What? Rina, what are you talking about?"

I repeated myself, but I was much louder this time. "I want to get married, baby!"

"Okay, and we will do that one day."

"One day is too far away, Harold. If you love me, you will marry me now."

"You know you would have to leave school if we got married now. Is that what you want?" Harold asked.

"Baby, I just want to be with you. I want to be your wife. Please, marry me." Closing my eyes, I prayed for my desired response from him.

Silence took over our conversation for a few seconds.

"Okay, then, baby. I will come home this weekend, and we can let your family know that we are getting married.

"I love you, Harold."

"I love you, too, Rina. Now, please, go to class."

I hung up the phone, feeling like a huge weight had been lifted off of me. Now the only thing I had to worry about was telling Mother Clara that I was dropping out of school and getting married. However, telling her would be so much better than enduring living with her for months during the summer.

•••

"I'm coming home tomorrow, Gwen," I announced, expecting to hear her respond in excitement.

"Okay," Gwen replied.

For the last few months, every time I called Gwen, she didn't have much conversation for me. I asked her multiple times if something was bothering her, but she only told me that she was fine. I felt an enormous amount of guilt for leaving her in that Godforsaken house by herself, but I wanted to better myself, and going to school was the way to do that. Even though I was about to drop out to get married, I could always go back at some point.

"Harold will be with me."

"Okay," Gwen replied again.

"Gwen, I have some really big news, and I want to tell you first."

Gwen didn't respond, so I continued.

"Harold and I are getting married!" I exclaimed.

Again, I was met with silence.

"Did you hear me?" I asked, wondering if the phone had suddenly disconnected.

"Yeah, I heard you. Why, Rina?"

"Because we love each other. I thought you would be happy for me." I was surprised Gwen was not as thrilled as I was at my big news.

"Rina, you already left me. Now you are telling me you never coming back?"

"Gwen, it's not like that,"

"I gotta go. Mother Clara is calling me."

"Wait, Gwen," I started. Before I could finish, she hung up the phone.

I was upset Gwen felt like I had left her. But at some point, I had to do something for me. At first, that was going off to college. But now, it was getting married. Once Harold and I were living together, Gwen could come stay with us. I could truly get her away from that house and everyone in it. I was going to prove to her that I would not leave her like Ruth Ann.

Chapter 14

Gwen

My days and nights ran together. Days passed, and then months, and before I could think about it, it had been three years since my child was ripped from my womb. I still felt the same intense pain as if it had just happened yesterday. I was numb, and I stopped fighting. My days consisted of going to school, coming home, and doing my chores. I avoided Mother Clara as much as humanly possible as I counted down the time until my high school graduation and when I would be able to go off to school like Rina. That thought was the only thing that got me through the nights when Satan entered my room and stripped any little bit of goodness from me that I desperately tried to hold onto. However, at this point, I believed I had no decency left inside of me. So, I drowned my pain in food and sweets I took from the kitchen when Mother Clara was asleep. That was the only thing that comforted me and felt good. I prayed the more weight I gained, the less likely anyone would want to touch me.

Ever since Mother Clara had learned about Billy and me, he was no longer allowed at the house or the club. Uncle Dale and

Uncle Lee made sure they let him know he was not welcomed anymore. And if he ever came over, he would not depart in one piece. Not only did I suffer the loss of my child, but I lost the one person who had made me feel loved.

I hung up the phone with Rina, and the words, "I'm getting married," swirled around in my head and caused sadness to settle in my chest. Not only had I been anticipating the day I would be leaving for the same college as Rina, but I also knew I would be truly protected once I was with her. If Rina had been with me and came home that day like she was supposed to a few years ago, I felt with all my being I would still have my baby. She could have saved my child and me from Mother Clara. Since she had been gone, I felt deserted here by myself. Once Rina got a job near her college, she stopped coming home as much on the weekends, leaving me feeling even more abandoned and miserable.

I stared at the knife sitting on my bed. Earlier today, as I was cleaning up the club with Mother Clara, I found the small pocketknife lying on the edge of the bar. I grabbed it before anyone else saw it and pushed it deep into my pants pocket. I thought about using it on Uncle Lee if he came back in my room late at night. But now that I gazed at it on my bed, other thoughts entered my head. I grabbed the blue handle on the butterfly knife and ran my fingers over the dents and marks it had. Flipping it open, exposing the sharp blade, I thought about how easy it would be to end it all right now. Whatever was on the other side could not possibly be worse than what I endured on this Earth. I ran the blade across my arm and felt how sharp it was. I was tired and wanted it to be over. I wanted to be with my child that was taken from me. I slowly placed the blade on my wrist.

"Gal, git in here!" Mother Clara's voice traveled from the kitchen into my bedroom, completely taking my attention from the knife and what I was about to do. I knew better than to take too long seeing what Mother wanted. I immediately closed the knife, dropped it on my bed, and ran to the kitchen.

I stopped directly in front of Mother Clara as a look of disgust covered her face. "Ya fat ass still think ya cute, don't ya?"

I was smart enough to know that wasn't a question Mother really wanted me to answer. She stared at me a moment longer and sucked her teeth. "Thinking dat way gonna get ya belly swole up again. Just like ya mammie. Wash up those pots from the club and gone to bed."

Grateful that my presence didn't bring another beating, I quickly did as Mother requested. I was now more determined to go through with what I planned. I would rather be anywhere other than this house. If that meant burning in the lake of fire that Aunt Marie warned us of, then I would gladly dive in headfirst.

I dried off the last glass, placed it in the cupboard, and ran back to my room. The knife sat on my bed, begging me to use it. I plopped down beside it and slowly picked it up again, turning it around and around in my hands. As soon as I exposed the blade, I heard the phone ring. I didn't want the ringing phone to disturb Mother, so I promptly ran to the kitchen to answer it.

"Hello," I answered, anxious to get back to my task at hand.

"Hey, Gwen, this is Rina."

"Hey, I was about to go to bed," I lied, not wanting to talk to my sister again. She was getting married and leaving me. I didn't have any more words for her.

"Gwen, I love you, and I will never leave you," she said as if she could read my mind.

I couldn't say anything and before I knew it, tears slipped down my cheeks.

"Gwen, you are not alone. You will never be alone. I love you, sister."

"I love you, too, Rina," I whispered.

"Go to bed, and I will be home soon, okay?"

"Okay."

I hung up the phone and dragged myself back to my room. The knife was still on my bed. But this time, I didn't want to use it. I picked it up and placed it underneath my mattress. Rina had saved me again.

Chapter 15

Beatrice

When I was younger, being alone never concerned me. Even when my mother was still alive, I was by myself most of the time. But this type of solitude was different. It was a haunting desolation that sent chills down my spine and tugged at my soul. It was the type of seclusion that made me want to gravitate to anything or anyone that could take away the void or fill up some of the empty parts of my heart. Unfortunately, this isolation led me to Gregg and my addiction.

I was three years out of high school and now living on my own in the same apartment complex I had grown up in. Thanks to staying with Ms. Ann and her keeping an eye on me after my mother's death, I was able to get a job with one of her nieces at a collection agency. I spent all my days calling customers, trying to get them to pay their bills, and then came home to an empty apartment. Ms. Ann had passed away a few months ago. Between her and my mom, they had been the only family close to me.

"Hey, Bea, how ya been?" Gregg asked as I was sitting down in the breakroom to eat my lunch.

At thirty-one, Gregg was around ten years older than me and had been working at our company for a little over six months now. His dirty reddish complexion and multiple blemishes on his face made him highly unattractive, so I tried to avoid him as much as possible. However, he always spoke to me whenever we saw one another. I was not interested in making new friends or even talking to people I was not familiar with, so a simple "hello" and "I'm fine" were all I would offer him.

"I'm fine," I mumbled, without looking up from the ham sandwich I had fixed for my lunch. Instead of just speaking and walking away like he usually did, Gregg pulled out the chair at the table and sat down across from me. Glancing at him and then back at my sandwich, I wasn't sure what to say or even if I wished to say something.

"So, you been here a while, huh?" he asked, opening up the barbeque potato chips he had purchased from the vending machine. I didn't care to involve myself in any small talk, so I simply nodded.

Ignoring my obvious failure to start a conversation, he continued to talk. "What ya got planned for this weekend?"

"Nothing," I replied, still staring at my sandwich.

"Not even a little mary jane?" Gregg whispered, sliding his chair next to mine. At this point, he was so close I could smell the chips on his breath. His proximity made me extremely uncomfortable and caused me to lean back in my chair. Even though I was uneasy, I was more startled at how upfront he was about smoking. There was only one person at my company who knew about my habit, and that was Tony. Tony and I were in the same training class. One day, I overheard him talking to another girl in our class about smoking. He noticed my apparent interest and had been my supplier ever since. I trusted Tony to an extent, well enough to believe he wouldn't tell that I got weed from him. Not only would that jeopardize me, but it would be trouble for him as well.

"What did you say?" I asked Gregg, hoping Tony hadn't been running his mouth about my extracurricular activities outside of work.

"It's okay, baby girl. Me and Tony work together if ya know what I mean," Gregg explained. He winked at me as he stuffed another chip into his mouth.

"I'm good," I replied, avoiding Gregg's eyes. I was pissed Tony had told anyone my business, even if he and Gregg supposedly ran together.

Gregg took a piece of paper and pen out of his pocket and scribbled his number on it. Then, he slid it over to me and stood from the table. "If you change your mind, just call me anytime."

I grabbed the piece of paper and stuffed it in my pants pocket. I had no intentions of using it, but I didn't want anyone else seeing he had given me his number. I didn't talk to anyone at my job and didn't want them in my business. That's how it had been since I started, and I wanted to keep it that way.

●●●

I suddenly woke up and stared off into the darkness of my apartment. After working twelve hours, it was common for me to fall asleep on my couch. But today, I didn't remember even closing my eyes.

I glanced at the old sofa that my mom and I had for years. The same couch that was once stained with my father's blood was reupholstered and taking up space in my living room. The thoughts of my parents didn't come to me at the same time, but this evening was different. As much as I was without my mother when she was living, I never felt as alone as I did now. Every day the feeling controlled me more and more. Smoking marijuana often helped dismiss the thoughts temporarily. But eventually, after my high was gone, the feelings would return.

I tried to go back to sleep. But every time I closed my eyes, I saw my mother's face. The talk we had the day she told me she was dying replayed in my head. As much as I wanted to show her I made something of myself, I knew I was failing. I had no real career path, and I hated the job I was at now. I had no friends, and the only family I did have, I made a vow to my mom to never trust them. All I had was me.

I needed something to make her disappear, something to make her go away, at least for the moment. I picked up my cell phone and scrolled until I found Tony's name. It didn't take long since I didn't have that many numbers in my phone anyway.

"Ay, yo. What's good, ma?" Tony answered on the second ring.

"I need something," I replied. He would know exactly what I desired, so there was no need to go into too much over the phone.

"I'm out of town, Bea. But I will send my man, Gregg, over. He got you."

Before I could object, the phone went silent. I really didn't want someone other than Tony to come over, especially not Gregg, after our encounter at work earlier. But it seemed like I didn't have much of a choice. Hopefully, he would get here soon, so the thoughts of my mother would disappear along with any other memories I had.

•••

Sleep had won again while I waited for Gregg to deliver my anticipated package. No one ever visited me other than Tony every once in a while. Therefore, I assumed it was Gregg once I heard a loud knock on my door. I planned to invite him in, take what he had for me before he even sat down, and push him back out of the door.

I opened the door and was surprised to see Gregg dressed in a navy-blue button-down dress shirt and dark brown khaki pants. He didn't seem nearly as unappealing as he had earlier. I opened the door wider, inviting him in.

"I was shocked when my man told me ya wanted me to come over," Gregg said, smirking at me.

"I didn't exactly ask for you," I replied, pointing toward the couch so he could sit down. Since he wasn't as revolting as he was at work, I decided not to rush him off so quickly. The alternative to him being here was me being alone, and I'd had enough of that, at least for tonight.

"Well, you may not have called me, but I'm glad he sent me." Gregg winked again like he had done earlier at work.

"Whatcha got?" I asked, suddenly feeling uncomfortable. I sat down on the opposite end of the couch as Gregg pulled out a small bag of the green stuff that immediately made my mouth water.

"Smell that," he ordered as he handed me the bag.

The aroma of the plant that would erase all memories of my mother caused a huge grin to spread across my face.

"Yeah, that's the good stuff, ma," Gregg said, watching me.

I nodded, agreeing with him, and slid the bag back toward him. "Nah, baby girl, that's all you."

"But Tony usually only gives me half this amount. I don't have enough for the whole bag."

"Just call it a gift." Gregg winked again.

Frightened where this was going, I decided to decline what he was offering. "It ain't that kind of party, Gregg. I pay Tony for what I can afford, and that's it," I said, hoping that he understood what I was saying.

Ignoring my statement, Gregg glanced around my room. Finally, his eyes rested on my dining room table.

"Mind if I use your table for a sec," he asked, still not responding to my last statement.

"Sure, but do you get what I was trying to say?"

"Calm down, ma. I get you." Gregg stood from the couch and walked over to the table. He took a seat and pulled out another bag from his pocket. However, this one didn't have the familiar plant I was used to seeing. Instead, this bad contained a white substance I couldn't make out from the couch.

Gregg noticed me staring at him. He winked again. "Come join me."

Curiosity replaced my uneasiness, and I did as he had suggested. Sitting across from him at my small wobbling black table that could only comfortably fit two people, I stared as he spread the white powdery substance onto the table and then formed it into a line.

"You gonna let me do this alone?" Gregg asked as he took a dollar bill out of his pocket. I watched as he put it to his nose and sniffed the white stuff up in one motion. I had seen this done in movies but never up close, and personal like right now. My first thought was to refuse. But just as I was about to, the image of my mother popped into my head again. Tonight, for some reason, I just couldn't stop seeing her.

"Bea," Gregg called, snapping me out of my obvious daze. He handed me the dollar and formed another line. But this time, directly in front of me.

"This will make you forget everything," he said as if he could read my thoughts.

I took the dollar from him. As I put it to my nose, I hoped it would indeed, at least for the night, make my mother vanish and make me forget.

Chapter 16

ClaRina

April 2000

(Thirty Years Later)

I stood in front of my bathroom mirror and brushed my hair toward the top of my head in a bun like I had seen Mother Clara do countless times. The thought of my grandmother caused me to pause for a second. She was dying. Last night, Mother Clara's nurse, Vanessa, called to notify me that she was on hospice care and would not be with us too much longer. Many times, when I was younger, I had wished death upon her. Now that it was becoming a reality, I did not know how to feel. A part of me wanted the memories of my childhood to wither away with her. Perish and be forgotten. The other part just longed to know if she ever really loved my sisters and me. And to be honest, I wondered how she had lived as long as she had, anyway. To be ninety-seven years old and still able to talk and think clearly was not a small feat. I guess the saying evil never dies had some validity to it.

"Harold, your blue shirt and tie are pressed and hanging up."

I waited a few seconds for his reply. "Thanks, dear," soon followed.

I reapplied a little more eyeliner and again fixed my bun. Tiny gray hairs were popping up around the edges once more. Grabbing my cell phone that sat between my double sinks, I typed a reminder to call Jennie for a hair appointment. I despised when my gray would start to show. The older I got, the more I had to see my hairstylist to dye my hair. Staring at myself in the mirror, I felt my makeup could use a little help today.

My mood was affecting everything, even the colors I chose to highlight my face. I placed my phone back down, grabbed my favorite Ruby Woo red lipstick, and traced my lips with it. Finally, a smile replaced the melancholy frown that had appeared earlier.

I walked out of my bathroom into my large walk-in closet to search for the perfect outfit for my meeting today. Today was the day I presented my ideas to my boss and the board of directors at my job. I was a social worker and manager at a disability office. For twenty-three years, I have thoroughly enjoyed my career. Even though I would be retiring soon, my career fulfilled me. It was my passion to help others. Deciding on my heather gray pantsuit, I hung it on the door. Tightening the belt on my black silk robe, I ran downstairs to meet my husband at the door. I surely could not miss Harold's departure. He left an hour before I did. Every morning since we had been married, I stood at the door and kissed him goodbye.

This had been our routine for almost thirty years now, not just habit. But for Harold, it was mandatory.

"Have a wonderful day." His salt and pepper beard brushed against my cheek as I stood on my tiptoes to plant a kiss on his full lips.

"You, too. Make sure you blow them away at your meeting today. And, please, pay the light bill," he replied.

"Yes, baby, what time will you be home?" I asked. He walked toward his recently purchased white Mercedes Benz.

Without looking back, he calmly replied, "It's Friday."

His nonchalant answer to my question was normal. I didn't care to respond. Instead, I just closed the door to our 8,000-square foot home and hurried back upstairs, so I could finish getting ready for work.

I loved what I did but being a social worker could not afford us the lavish lifestyle we had maintained for so long. Harold owned his own construction company and built houses similar to the one we called our home.

As I continued to get dressed, I thought back on the day I first met Harold and had instantly fallen in love with him. I was a freshman, and he was a senior at Claflin University in Orangeburg, South Carolina. Even though he was in a fraternity, he was one of the more low-key brothers of Alpha Phi Alpha, Inc. The first time I saw his gorgeous smile was at one of their on-campus fraternity parties. I was standing off to the side, chatting with my cousin, Will, who happened to be Harold's line brother. Harold took one look at me, and boldly told me that he was going to make me his woman. His arrogance, sprinkled in with charm, caused me to feel butterflies. He was the first man who had ever made me feel loved, and, sure enough, I became his. The rest, as many would say, is history.

I slipped into my black pumps; I heard my phone buzzing in the bathroom. Since it was only 7:15, I had one guess who was calling—my sister Gwen.

I ran into the bathroom and answered. "I will be there in twenty minutes," I said, hanging up before my sister had a chance to respond.

Telling Gwen about Mother Clara's pending death was on my to-do list for today. Calling her on the phone and informing her of this last night was not an option. Gwen was forty-six on paper but still a fifteen-year-old girl emotionally and mentally. I was certain that hearing anything about our grandmother would dredge up memories Gwen would not be able to handle alone. Maybe it was my fault for coddling her all these years. But growing up, I had to protect her. However, I never would have guessed the sheltering and consistent support of her would be never-ending.

I opened the door to my midnight blue BMW and suddenly felt dizzy. Dizzy spells welcomed me in the mornings and tucked me in at night more than I cared to admit. With so much on my plate, I did not have the time or energy to see my physician. My self-diagnosis was that between being the doting wife, worrying about my now grown daughter, who had just moved in with her boyfriend, and still being at Gwen's every beck and call, the dizzy moments had to be because of stress.

Pulling out of my circular driveway, I noticed Meadow Pines seemed a bit quieter than normal this morning. Harold and I had been residing in this peaceful neighborhood for thirteen years, and I enjoyed living here. Most of my neighbors were pleasant and rather friendly. Since we had been here, we hadn't had one problem.

Today, however, was somewhat unusual. No neighbors waved as I drove by. No residents picked up their morning newspapers to see the latest and greatest happenings. The trees stood motionless and patient as if awaiting a deep secret to be unlocked. The still of the community drifted my thoughts back to Mother Clara.

Charleston, South Carolina, had been my residence since I graduated from college. After I moved here to this large city, Gwen soon followed. Surrounded by beautiful beaches and historic scenery, my city was one that I was proud to call my home.

I glided my car onto the highway. Fifteen minutes later, I pulled onto my sister's street. I drove into Terrence Heights and parked directly in front of Gwen's apartment building. I was a few minutes early and texted her that I was outside. After ten minutes, I texted her again. Every morning, it was the same thing.

"I'm coming!" Gwen hollered as if it was four in the afternoon and not early morning. She stood on her doorstep, about to close the door and turned back around.

"Come on, please," I said even though Gwen couldn't hear me. As soon as she walked down the stairs of her second-floor apartment, I thought, "*This could not possibly be the same girl from when we were younger who once obsessed over her looks so much that she would cry when she thought her hair wasn't good enough for school.*"

Gwen appeared as if she had just rolled out of bed five minutes before my arrival. Her thick long reddish-brown hair was slightly brushed back in a ponytail, and her uniform had enough wrinkles to where I questioned if she even owned an iron. One side of her gray post office shirt was slightly tucked in, and the other side was barely reaching her pants to cover up her multiple stomach rolls. She meandered down her stairs like she did not have a care in the world.

"Sorry, sis!" Gwen said, struggling to get her oversized frame into my car and then slamming the door. Sweat beads surrounded her forehead and covered her nose.

Usually, I would fuss about her presence and her attire, but my thoughts of Mother Clara were heavy on my mind. After riding in odd silence for about ten minutes, I glanced at my sister staring out of the window.

"What's wrong?" I asked, turning onto the interstate and merging in front of an eighteen-wheeler. Traffic was picking up. I planned to try to leave early enough to avoid the morning rush hour. But as always, Gwen's tardiness had dismissed that idea.

Every morning, Gwen was a chatterbox. But today, she had barely said anything other than she was sorry. Last night, I called our sister, Beatrice, who lived in New York, to tell her about Mother Clara, but I was sure she wouldn't tell Gwen. For one, Gwen and Bea never talked, and the reason for that was because they could not stand one another.

"Ri Ri, this is the last time. I promise."

I took my eyes off my sister and put them back on the road. Once her infamous lie bounced upon my ears, I knew what else was coming. When Gwen started her sentences off, "This is the last time," I could be assured that asking for money would follow. It seemed like the last time for this request never came.

"Come on, Gwen, not this again." My need to scold Gwen was overwhelming more than any other time due to her constant begging and Mother's current health conditions. Regardless of how much I fussed, it never did any good. The tears would soon follow, and I could definitely do without her reverting to her adolescent whining and crying ways.

I had taken responsibility for her since before I could remember. The one time I was not there for her as a child haunted me to this day, and I made sure that never happened again. I made sure she did not experience the bad things I endured. And in some ways, that crippled her. No, not some ways, all ways.

"How much, Gwen?"

"It's five-hundred this time," she said, without looking at me.

"When you need it?"

"Today, if possible."

I did not even ask what it was for this time because it would not matter. Whatever bill or emergency Gwen had; I was the only one who could help with it. All I could do was shake my head, at not only Gwen but also at myself. We had perfected the continuous cycle of robbing Peter to pay Paul. However, in this case, I was Peter, and Paul was Gwen's light bill, cable bill, and my nephews. Unfortunately, like Peter, I would never see my money back.

As we pulled into the post office parking lot, I reached in my Brahmin brown leather purse and pulled out five crisp one-hundred-dollar bills.

This money's purpose was to pay the light bill at the other house. That meant because I was always burdened with taking care of my sister, I would have to change my own plans and stop by the bank after work. Then I would have to go by the electric company, which was across town. I didn't have a choice in the matter, though. Today was Friday. If I didn't pay that bill, Harold would surely know.

"Here." I handed the money to my sister.

"I promise this is the last time," she said.

"Go to work, Gwen."

I drove off without even telling my sister about Mother Clara. The only thing that consumed me now was getting off in time to get to the bank and pay the light bill. The hell that would follow not completing that one task was something I never wanted to go through again.

Chapter 17

Beatrice

I slammed my front door and stared at the clothes, shoes, dirty dishes, and papers that cluttered the living room of my small one-bedroom apartment.

"Oh, no, you don't! Die!" I screamed, stomping on the roach, attempting to hide under my couch. He probably was on his way to join his family. *At least he had one*, I thought. I continued to look around the filth of my apartment.

"This shit is fucking ridiculous! Ricky!"

I was almost certain my deadbeat boyfriend was in bed, enjoying his second afternoon nap, while our other unwelcomed roommates had an ongoing shindig in our living room.

"Ricky!" I called out again, stepping over the pile of dirty clothes to get to my bedroom. Ricky met me at the door, dressed in only his boxers. His muscular ebony chest glistened as if he had just rubbed down with an entire bottle of baby oil.

"Don't start, baby, just come here," he said, grabbing me around my waist.

I tried to push him off me but seeing him in his boxers while his manhood was somewhat ready to attack made me weak. I allowed him to kiss my neck, which was my spot. Before I knew it, he had undressed me, and we were tumbling around on the half-made bed and on top of a stack of dirty clothes.

After all the stress from work and walking into this dump, I needed something to take the edge off. Ricky pulled me on top of him. I guided him inside of me, rocked back and forth, and I remembered why I had put up with his no-good ass for so long. His sex was the best I had ever had in my whole life. I craved him no matter how much I had to put up with.

"Ricky, I'm about to c…" I stuttered as I had the most intense orgasm.

Ricky flipped me over on my stomach and slipped back inside of me. His gentle slow movements became faster and more intensified by the moment. Ricky pounded into me, grunting, and moaning until finally, he began to tremble. After a few seconds, he collapsed on top of me. Sweating and still on a high from releasing all my frustrations from the day, I rolled over and stared at Ricky. He quickly stood and began to put his boxers back on. He then picked up his jeans from the floor and began to get fully dressed.

"You got some money, Bea?"

His question knocked me out of my state of euphoria and prompted me to get up and dressed.

Ricky walked out of the bedroom, looking down at his phone as I followed him.

"Are you serious?" I asked, feeling my frustrations suddenly coming back. "So, your plan was to fuck me and then get some money out of me?"

I held my breath for a few seconds before I spoke again. I was so sick of this damn man. I didn't trust him as far as I could see him. I had been dealing with him off and on for five years and still could not figure out why I continued to be with him. There was absolutely nothing good about him, except the soul snatching orgasm he had just given me. I was ten years his senior and being with him kept me youthful. It also kept me broke, tired, and annoyed. But he was the only person I had, if I could call it that.

Ricky ignored my question. "Oh, did you pay the rent last month? Ya gotta eviction notice sitting over there." He pointed at the kitchen table, then looked back down at his phone again.

I rolled my eyes. Enough was enough. "Ricky, I'm too old for this shit." I sighed.

My comment was met with his laughter. "Oh, yeah? You got something better?" he asked, still chuckling. "Your ass wasn't tired a few minutes ago when you were screaming my name."

Turning my back to him, I looked around my apartment that had been my home for the last eleven years. The rent went up every year, but it was still the same tiny, almost unlivable run-down place that it had always been. Ever since my rent had skyrocketed to twenty-one-hundred dollars a month a year ago, I was greeted with an eviction notice each time. Somehow, I managed to get the money together right before they kicked my ass out.

I turned to face Ricky again to express my disgust with him and our living conditions. His backhand connected with my face and spun me around. Blood oozed from my mouth. Some might have been amazed that just thirty minutes ago, I was making love to this man, and now he had just slapped the shit out of me, but I was not. We fought almost weekly, but I was at my breaking point. I was not going to continue to take this from him.

Ricky laughed again, "I gave you this good dick, now I need some money."

I mustered up all the power I had in my small, five-one, 135-pound frame and pounced on him, almost sending him to the ground. I used my long-pointed nails to dig into his bearded face and rip as much of it as I possibly could.

"Get off me, Bea!" Ricky screamed. He tugged and tried to pull me off, but I had a fierce grip on him and locked my legs around his waist. This would be the last time he ever put his hands on me. I was tired of fighting and, more so, just sick of his trifling ass.

A few months ago, I had found out he was cheating on me again. The woman he was seeing sent me a message on Facebook and a video of them having sex. I cursed him out. We fought, but that was it. He stayed, and I stopped fussing. I never forgave him—like I stated before, he was all I had.

I had no friends nor family. Well, not any family here in New York. My mom was all I had, and now that she was gone, Ricky was it.

My sisters, who I barely knew, lived in South Carolina along with the rest of my mom's family. The last time I visited that little hick country town was over thirty years ago. My mother advised me to never go back, and I obeyed.

At different jobs over the years, I made friends here and there. But the friendships never lasted. I didn't trust people; I never let anyone get too close to me. I got what I needed from them, whether it was money, material things, or a ride, and when they attempted to get more acquainted, I quickly cut them off. My mother trained me to never trust anyone, and she did not teach me a lot. But that one thing stuck to me, and I followed it. There was only one person I had ever completely trusted, which was my childhood friend, Sheila. However, her mother stopped allowing her to spend time with me once my mother passed. Then a year later, her family relocated to the west coast.

"Just get out! You ain't did shit for me but fuck me, and I am tired of living like this!" I screamed, still holding on to him for dear life.

"I ain't going no damn where," Ricky growled. He maintained his balance and finally pulled me off of him, throwing me down to the floor. As he was coming toward me, there was a loud knock at the door.

"Police!" a man's thunderous voice rang out from the other side of my door.

Ricky stopped dead in his tracks. "When did you call the damn police?"

"I didn't! Probably one of our nosy neighbors that heard us fighting again," I said, struggling to stand up.

The pounding on the door made me switch from looking at Ricky to the door. "We gotta answer it."

"Bea, you better not put me in jail again," Ricky walked toward me, pointing his finger in my face.

"If you go and never come back, I won't." I figured this was my best bet to get Ricky to leave me alone. If he was arrested one more time for domestic violence, he was looking at a year or two in jail.

"Aight, aight, just open the door, and tell 'em we were playing or something," Ricky begged.

I wiped my nose with the back of my hand and opened the door. Standing on the other side, getting ready to knock again, were two white, uniformed cops.

"Ma'am, we received a call about a disturbance."

The tall skinny red-headed cop, who could not have been a day over twenty, looked at me in disgust as if he wanted to say he knew a black woman would answer the door. As he talked, the pale short chunky cop, standing next to him who looked as if he was carrying shopping bags under his eyes, tried to peer around into my apartment.

I stepped to the side and blocked his view of the inside of my home. "Sir, I am not sure which one of my neighbors called you, but there is no disturbance here," I said in my best white girl voice. The same voice I used all day while talking to my customers on the phone.

"Well, ma'am, please keep whatever it is down, so your neighbors won't have to call us again," the red-headed cop insisted.

"Will do." I gave him a fake smile and slowly closed my door.

I turned around and stared at Ricky. Ricky's bald head was freshly shaven, and with his designer jeans and black collared shirt on, he looked as if he had money instead of the freeloader, I knew him to be.

"You wanna go to jail, or you wanna go home?" I asked, mocking Denzel Washington from the movie *Training Day*.

Ricky walked past me without saying a word. He opened the door and walked out, not once turning around. That day, I knew it was completely over between him and me. Now I had to figure out how to come up with two thousand dollars in two days with only one-hundred-fifty-six bucks in my bank account.

Chapter 18

Gwen

"I can help the next person in line." I forced a smile as a petite older lady with a shabby gray wig pinned to her head, handed me a small package. I glanced at the time on my terminal as it flashed 3:35 p.m. In less than an hour, I would be out of this place for the weekend. I could not wait to be free of work for a few days.

"Tanya, I'm going to the bathroom," I informed my co-worker, who stood at the terminal a few feet away from me.

Tanya glanced at me and then continued to talk to the Asian man inquiring about how long it would take for his package to reach California. I finished the lady's transaction, threw the package in the bin behind me, and sprinted toward the restroom.

My cell phone was in my pocket, even though we weren't supposed to have phones on the floor. However, I always kept mine close. I needed to text Chris and let him know I had the money.

I hated deceiving my sister, but I had no choice. Rina had just paid my rent on the first. I knew getting more money out of her would be damn near impossible. Not only had she given me nine hundred dollars for my rent, but she had also taken DeSean, Kareem, and Jaden shopping for school clothes. Even though I worked at the post office and made decent money, I was always broke. If I didn't give all my money away to Chris, I would have some for my bills and kids. However, Chris said he loved me, and I believed him. Whatever he needed, I would get it for him, even if that meant being dishonest to Rina. She owed me at least that anyway.

I quickly sent the text and rushed back to my station. The last thing I needed was Tanya bringing attention to how long I had been in the bathroom.

Her jealousy for me having tenure over her was louder than the lime green scarf loosely tied around the customer's neck now standing in front of me.

"Thought we were gonna have to come looking for you again," Tanya smirked, flipping her knotless braids, and showing off her engagement ring at the same time. If anything, I should have been envious of her instead of the other way around. Tanya's caramel skin was complemented with a cute smile, small waist, and big booty. Her boyfriend of two years had proposed to her a week ago, and she was constantly showing off her two-carat diamond engagement ring.

I ignored her petty comment and thought about Chris again. After what seemed like an eternity, I glanced at my phone. Thirty minutes until quitting time. Tonight, Chris would be elated that I was able to get him the money he needed. That meant he just might spend the entire night with me. If I were really lucky, perhaps, I would get a ring like Tanya's. I knew that was wishful thinking. But maybe, eventually, I would get what I desired from Chris.

I had finally found a man who said he loved me. As long as I was able to get him what he needed, he gave me what I yearned for, which was him. I wanted to be loved. I needed to be loved. No matter what, I was going to get exactly what I desired. No matter the cost.

•••

"Where you going?" I asked, wiping my mouth with the bottom of my black lingerie set. I grabbed on to the edge of my couch to pull myself up from the kneeling position I had spent the last thirty minutes in. I had just finished pleasing Chris orally and thought he was going to stay at least to reciprocate. He had never returned the favor before.

But he had promised me that if I could get him the cash he needed, he would show his gratitude in more ways than one and make love to me like never before. I was hoping this had included dining on me and gobbling me up like I was Thanksgiving dinner.

Chris always wanted oral sex when he came over. Since that was his only favorite thing to receive, he rarely allowed me any pleasure. Now and then, we would make love, but those times were few and far between. At first, he said he did not know how to handle a woman as large as me. After I begged and promised I would be gentle and show him exactly what I liked, he finally gave in. I attempted to make him as comfortable as possible, but the only time he could get an erection was when his penis was in my mouth. He admitted he enjoyed my oral skills so much he would rather stick with that. I obliged since having him over meant more to me than him actually sleeping with me. Of course, I had needs, but I wanted Chris around a lot more than worrying about what I was not getting physically.

"Chill, I'll be back." He stood, zipped up, and fastened his blue slacks.

Chris was always impeccably dressed. But tonight, he looked even more dapper in a pink Polo shirt and blue dress pants. His dreads were neatly done and hung loosely over his shoulders. I was used to seeing him dressed finely, but not as appealing as he was tonight. His style was just one more thing I adored about him. We had been dating for five months. I could honestly say I was in love. Even though it never took me long to fall in love, this time, it was different.

"But when? I cooked dinner," I pleaded, pointing over to the table of food that I was sure he saw when he walked into my apartment.

I planned a romantic evening since I knew Chris would be overly excited I had gotten the money for him. The reason he desperately needed the five hundred dollars was that he had gotten into a little trouble with gambling and had to have the extra cash to pay off his debt.

When he told me about his problem, he looked me straight in my eyes and told me how much he loved me. That was his first time speaking those words to me, so I knew I had to help him. I was more than grateful I could be there for him.

Ribeye steaks, baked potatoes, asparagus, potato salad, and homemade biscuits decorated my dining room table untouched and now cold. Duping Rina once again, I was able to get her to watch my kids, so Chris and I could be alone. And that was not a small feat because I had three young men who could eat anyone out of a house and home. My teenagers were a handful. I was surprised my sister agreed to watch them. But then again, she would do anything for me. I plotted and schemed to get Chris alone, and now I was just lonely.

Chris had left about fifteen minutes ago, but it seemed like an hour. I called his phone and didn't get an answer. Maybe he would be back soon, I hoped.

I placed the food in the oven and decided to watch TV to take my mind off of Chris and his disappearance. Since it looked as if I would be by myself for a while, I changed out of my nightie into some sweatpants and a shirt. I took a swig of the wine that had been sitting on the table awaiting me and Chris. I thought back on each one of my four son's fathers. My oldest son, Craig was in jail for the third time for selling drugs. I tried to be the best parent I could but regretfully I never learned exactly how. I had met his father when I went off to college at Claflin University. The only reason I had gone to school was because Rina was there. During my final semester as a freshman, I met Riley and fell in love. He took me on dates, sent me flowers, and told me that he would marry me one day. Seven months after dating, I became pregnant, and Riley disappeared. He didn't come back to school the next year, and all my phone calls went unanswered. I was alone and pregnant. I dropped out of school and moved in with Rina until I could get a job and my own place.

My stories with DeSean, Kareem, and Jaden's dads were pretty much the same. DeSean was my second to the oldest son and would be graduating high school this year. I wish I could say he would be receiving his diploma thanks to me however, I couldn't.

My focus was more on finding someone to love me so maybe in return I could love my boys better.

Before I knew it, two hours had passed, and Chris was still not back. I glanced at my phone, and it was now 10:30. Where could he be? I called his phone again with no answer. I was beginning to get worried. Maybe he had an accident or something. Should I go look for him? Just as I was about to get my jacket and head out the door to search for Chris, my phone started ringing.

I was so relieved when I saw Chris' name pop up on my screen. "Baby, I was so worried," I said as soon as I put the phone to my ear.

"Baby?"

"Hello?" I asked, glancing at my phone again. It was Chris' number. But surely, this was not Chris on the other end.

"Baby?" the woman asked again.

"Who is this? Where is Chris? Is he okay?"

"This is Chris' girlfriend. This is his cousin Gwen, right? The one that gave him the money to help us?"

"Girlfriend? Cousin? What the hell is going on?" I asked, shouting. Was this woman playing on my phone? "*I* am Chris' girlfriend!" I yelled. I gripped the phone tighter as sweat beads began to form on my forehead.

Before I had a chance to say anything else, the phone went silent. I called his number back; it went to voicemail. I called ten more times, and it still went to Chris' voicemail. This couldn't be happening. I had just given this man five hundred dollars. *Five hundred* of my sister's money. Not again, not again.

My mind went back to my last boyfriend, Nathan, and all the drama he had taken me through with using me, taking my money, and cheating. No, no, Chris was not like that. He told me he loved me! Chris told me that he wanted me, and I knew he was telling the truth.

He had to be telling the truth. It was not going to end like this! I grabbed my jacket, keys and headed out the door. Someone was going to give me some answers. I just prayed Rina had another five hundred dollars she was willing to give me just in case I needed it to get out of jail tonight like the two times before.

Chapter 19

ClaRina

I rolled over on my side and glanced at the alarm clock sitting on my nightstand. It flashed 10:00 in clear red numbers on the display. Saturday morning's presence was one over the years that I longed for and dreaded at the same time. It meant Harold would be returning soon. Saturday mornings for years would follow a long depressing Friday night of weeping and calling on God. Friday nights, at first, were heartbreaking. But after ten years of the same routine, I became accustomed to it. Instead of sobbing, I filled my Friday nights with mommy-daughter time. Now that Mia was grown, I had more time to myself. I would occupy my time by binge-watching my favorite shows on Netflix or reading a steamy romance novel. I did not dare ask Harold to stray away from his plans, even when some Friday nights loneliness would crawl into my room, wrap itself around my neck, and nearly strangle me to death. However, I was quickly reminded that living like this and wanting for nothing came at a price—a price I had been paying for over half of my marriage.

My normal Saturday mornings consisted of getting up no later than eight, tidying the house, and starting our weekly laundry. But, after talking to both my sisters yesterday about our perishing grandmother, I was drained physically and mentally. Gwen and Bea took the news exactly how I thought they would, casually and without much concern. Hidden emotions, I assumed, was their way of coping. I could only wonder how they really felt. Although they did not seem to show much interest in our grandmother's pending death, just thinking back to my childhood was more than enough to handle for myself. All I could do to get some rest was pour a few glasses of my favorite Chardonnay and pray that sleep would find me soon.

Since Harold was not back yet, I decided to get a few more hours of sleep. Hopefully, his night went well, and he would be in a pleasant mood. That would be one less thing to worry about. I hadn't even gotten the chance to tell him about Mother Clara's illness and last request, delivered to me through her nurse, of having my sisters and I visit her one last time.

Honestly, I wasn't even sure why I was taking on this responsibility. My grandmother was as atrocious to me as she was to my sisters. Even with all the dreadful memories, I still attempted to visit her and help as often as possible. Gwen thought I was completely insane to travel two hours at least two or three times a year to Timmonsville and clean up her house and take care of the grandmother who caused us so much misery when we were young. I guess, in my mind, it was my way of telling her no matter what she had put me through, she did not and could not break me. I would drive my car into the driveway of that old rickety white brick one-story house and get out, draped in my designer jeans and blouse.

My grandmother beat us, tore us down, and never showed us any love, but she did not destroy me. So, I cleaned her house, bought her groceries, and made sure she was taken care of.

As she got older, she wasn't as mean. We talked more, but she was still who she was, and a part of me felt sorry for her. Nonetheless, during the last few years, I had not visited Mother Clara as much as I used to. I resolved on just a phone call now and then to check on her. My frequent trips ended when the memories of my past became the actions of my present.

"Oh, God!" I screamed, trying to catch my breath. I had dozed off again and this time was awakened by a glass of ice-cold water being splashed in my face. At first, I thought I was dreaming. But as I opened my eyes and saw Harold standing in front of me with an empty red plastic cup in his hand, I knew this wasn't a dream. It was my somber reality.

"What the hell, Harold!" I sat up in the middle of the bed and tried to wipe my face with our satin bedsheets. "Why would you do that?" Water dripped from my hair, making my attempts to dry off senseless.

"It's noon, and you're still in the bed," he replied, calmly standing over me like the God he believed he was. "The laundry will not wash itself," Harold scoffed at me, and turned around to walk out of our bedroom. Before he stepped outside of the door, he turned around, "I will not repeat myself."

I can't say I was surprised by his actions. One would think that a man who had two women and two families would be satisfied after spending the night with his mistress. But, no, not my husband. When he was mad at her, I was the one who had to hurt. And when he was happy with her, I was the one who suffered because he had to come back home to me. Like I said before, this lifestyle came with a price.

•••

I put the last load of clothes in the dryer and walked downstairs to the family room. Even though I had a full night's rest, I was still exhausted. Over the past few months, I noticed that no matter how much sleep I had gotten the night before, fatigue still followed. Maybe it was time to visit my doctor to see if my iron was low or if I was undergoing another ailment.

As expected, my husband sat on our black leather couch with his favorite red coffee mug with *Best Father* in white letters printed on it, reading the newspaper. Mia had bought him the cup many years ago as a Father's Day gift, and he drank out of it every morning he was at home.

His legs were crossed, showing the blue and purple socks I had bought him for his birthday, along with the navy-blue dress slacks and sky-blue shirt, also purchased by me.

"Mother Clara is dying," I said to the back of Harold's head. I stood in the doorway, staring at him and waiting for his response.

He sat his newspaper down and turned around to look at me. "Baby, I am so sorry to hear that. Are you okay?"

I stared at him and shook my head. Not because Mother Clara was passing, but because this man, who just dumped a cup of cold water on me, was now talking to me like nothing had happened. He just called me baby and looked at me with concern displayed on his face. This was my life. This was my secret. My sisters were jealous of me. They believed I had the most devoted husband, the best marriage, and everything any woman could want. If they only knew the bipolar man I had been living with for thirty years, they would not want my life so bad. Harold had not always been this way. I often reflected on the life we had before him owning his own business and making millions. He was once a humble and kind person. But like so many others, money changed him into this power-hungry tyrant who felt he could do whatever he wanted without any consequences.

"She wants me and my sisters to visit her. I'm the only one that still talks to her, so I have been tasked with trying to get them to go see her."

"How is that working out?" Harold asked, picking his newspaper back up.

"You know, as long as I go, Gwen will go. I'm not sure about Bea."

"I hope you are able to get things together. Oh, I won't be here tonight, so that will give you time to handle your family business."

"But it's Saturday, Harold."

"I know what day it is," he growled, "Something came up."

I knew better than to argue with him once he said that. That "something" was his thirty-five-year-old mistress, Ebony.

Harold regained his composure and spoke again. "We will have Sunday."

"Okay," I replied.

"Are you going to change into something a little nicer?" Harold asked, making mention of the worn blue jeans and sweatshirt I had on. These were my Saturday around-the-house clothes.

Harold had seen them for years, so I wasn't sure what prompted him to address my clothing now. One thought, however, came to mind. He wanted me to dress more like his young girlfriend that he adored so.

"Sure," I responded.

"And you did pay the light bill, right?" he asked, peering at me from behind his paper.

"Yes, dear. Her lights will not be cut off."

I walked out of the family room with my sisters on my mind, replacing the thoughts of my husband, his other family, and the fact that I had to pay bills for both houses. For Mother Clara to request to see all of us was unexpected and piqued my curiosity. Those reasons alone were why my sisters and I needed to go. If nothing else, I had to get them to Timmonsville one last time.

Chapter 20

Beatrice

The sunlight blasted into my room like a cranky toddler in search of his mom and sadly reminded me that a new day had arrived. I purposely decorated my petite bedroom with blackout curtains, so the sun could not disturb my rest. But somehow, the light continuously seeped in. This morning, however, it invaded my room and took total control. Today was Saturday and my day off. Ricky had left a week ago, and I had not heard from him. This was not the first time he had left. But after two or three days away, he would usually come back. I was surprised and relieved at the same time.

Working all week had taken its toll on my body. It was not so much of the working part but trying to stay sober enough to perform my daily job functions. I turned on my side and tried to remember how much cash I had on me. Today was the final day to pay my rent. I still had not come up with the two thousand to keep me from being put out on the street. I didn't even have enough money to support my habit at this moment. But I knew if I had that, the thought of being homeless probably wouldn't have the same effect on me. I needed it after being on the phone with those dumb customers for twelve hours yesterday. I worked for a small cell phone company in their call center. My job was to listen to complaining customers all day and attempt to resolve their issues. The truth of the matter was that half of the time, there was no real solution to their problems. Either they had a raggedy phone or terrible plan. While at work, my vices were my cigarettes and a blunt I kept in my car for extreme purposes. For those moments when I had been on the phone with a customer for almost an hour, repeating myself, and they still did not understand. The blunt was my break in case of emergency; at least one time during the day, I needed it.

"What you got planned for your day off, Bea?" one of my obnoxious coworkers asked me before I left yesterday.

I turned to Gloria, the short thick chocolate girl sitting behind me. "I plan on getting some rest," I said before grabbing my purse from under my desk and heading out the door.

Just because she had given me a ride back and forth from work, she assumed we were friends and always wanted to hang out after work. However, I had no desire to interact with my coworkers once I walked out of this building. Little did her nosy ass know that I planned to get as high as I could with the little bit of money I had.

I was a functioning addict and had come to terms with that years ago. In and out of rehab for the last ten years, and the most I had stayed clean was almost six months. Then my memories would pour over into my dreams and cause me to binge for a few days.

The sunlight and now my phone were keeping me from resting. I refused to answer it or even look to see who the caller was, fearing it was my sister again. Rina was worried about me. But she had not endured what I had, or maybe I just wasn't strong enough to deal with it alone. I needed to self-medicate to make it through not just the day, but one minute to the next.

She had called me the night before telling me that my dying grandmother wanted to see me before taking her forever dirt nap.

"Why in the hell would I go visit that old woman?" I asked Rina, utterly confused as to the reason Mother Clara would even want to see me. She barely knew me. I didn't know her, and I was completely fine with keeping it that way.

Rina tried to persuade me, but her weak attempt fell on deaf ears last night. However, now that I thought about it and realized my cash flow was low, maybe it wasn't a bad idea to go see the old hag. If nothing else, perhaps she had some cash she was going to leave to us.

I mean, that is the least she could do. Die and leave me some money. I smiled at the thought of having an extra stash to do whatever I wanted.

Once I glanced at my ringing phone and saw that it was Rina calling again, my smile faded. She was the only sister who checked on me and the only family member I would talk to from time to time. I didn't care for Gwen, and I felt that was more than mutual on her part as well.

I ignored the call for the second time. Instead, I dialed one of my favorite numbers.

"Sexy, Bea! What you need?" Damon asked.

"You already know. You got me or what?"

"Ricky lame ass can't get you straight?" Damon chuckled.

"You don't worry 'bout him. Let me come over and give you some of what he was getting, so you can give me what I need."

"Get your sexy ass over here then, Bea."

•••

"Damon?" I whispered, trying to determine if he was asleep. After our second round, I was sure I had put him in a sex-induced coma, but I had to make certain. I watched him snore for a few minutes; then I decided he indeed was in a deep sleep.

I carefully sat up, so I would not wake him and climbed out of his queen-sized sleigh bed. The tiny lamp on the nightstand by the bed was still on, giving me enough light to see where I was going.

Damon had been my dealer for years now and was someone I could count on to regularly trade sex for drugs whenever my money was running low. However, this time, I needed a little more from him.

I glanced around the bedroom and was relieved when I saw Damon's wallet on the nightstand. I was desperate and didn't know what else to do.

Tiptoeing over to where his wallet was placed, I grabbed it. *Luck must really be on my side,* I thought. I took eight hundred dollars and sat his wallet back down. Beside his wallet as if it was waiting for me and me only was a small bag of the white powder that made me call Damon in the first place. Even though Damon had already gifted me with one bag in exchange for my time, I didn't see the harm in taking another one. I grabbed the drugs and stuffed them in my pants pocket. "Now let me get the hell out of here." I slipped my clothes back on and bolted for the door.

•••

I ignored another call from Damon. I always went to meet him and never invited him over to my house; therefore, he did not know where I lived and could not find me—at least not yet. By now, from his obscene messages, he realized I had stolen his money and drugs, and he was livid. My phone beeped again; another threatening text message came through. It would not be long before Damon and his goons found me, so I had to think of something fast. The plan to steal from him and pay my rent was not working out the way I thought it would. I still didn't have enough money to keep from being evicted, and now Damon was on my back.

My phone rang again. "Shit!" I screamed. I glanced at my phone, assuming that Damon was calling once more. Instead, it was just Rina.

"Hello," I answered on the third ring.

"Hey, Bea, how are you?"

"Hey, Rina, I'm good. What's up?" I asked, wanting Rina to hurry up and tell me why she called, so I could go back to figuring out what to do about Damon. I glanced at my phone; another threat from Damon came through.

"I was calling again to see if you made a decision about flying down to see Mother Clara. You don't have to pay for anything. If you say yes, I'll buy your plane ticket now."

This was perfect! I needed to get out of town quickly. Even though I could not have cared less about the old woman dying, this would solve my Damon problem.

"You can buy it today?"

"Sure! I'm so excited that you're coming!"

Rina continued rambling on and on. I tuned her out and thought about how I had a pocket full of money and a way to leave without Damon knowing. At least that one problem would be solved. I also still had enough to get me high so I would just worry about the rest later.

Chapter 21

ClaRina

"I think it would do you some good to get away for a while. I really miss our time together." I tried to persuade Mia to go to Timmonsville with me for the weekend.

She moved out of the house a year ago and was now living with her boyfriend, Maurice. My daughter had always been my sanity in my complicated world, and the bond between us was unbreakable. I must admit there were times I was a little overbearing. However, I felt I had to be. I never wanted Mia to feel like I did growing up. I didn't want her to feel unloved and abandoned, so I showed her at every turn that she was the best part of me. I had to learn how to love and love the right way. In the first few years, when I met Harold, he taught me what true love felt like. For years, I held on to who he used to be, not realizing the person he had slowly become.

Now that Mia had her own place, I barely saw her. Each time we planned to have lunch or dinner together, she canceled, claiming she wasn't feeling good or had to study for a test. Mia was in her senior year of college, majoring in nursing, and I was beyond proud of her. However, her choice of men did not make me stick my chest out and boast about it. Mia was as smart as a whip, as the saying goes. But somewhere along the way, her common sense didn't grow as fast as the knowledge she obtained.

I met Maurice twice before Mia sprung on Harold and me that she was moving in with him. He was as polite as to be expected when meeting his girlfriend's parents. But the sneakiness I saw in his eyes did not sit too well with me. Of course, Harold paid no attention and told me I was overreacting as usual, but I didn't trust the young man.

I thought Harold would have been more protective over his oldest daughter, but I suppose he had too many other things to worry about, such as his other children.

"Mom, I just can't make it this weekend," Mia insisted.

"I haven't seen you in so long, Pumpkin." Anytime I wanted to soften Mia up or had bad news to tell her, I called her my favorite pet name.

"Don't start, Ma. I'll see ya soon. Talk to you later. Love you." Mia hung up before I had a chance to respond.

I needed to at least lay my eyes on my daughter. So, before I would get on the road tomorrow, I planned to make an unexpected stop at her apartment. Normally, I wouldn't do that. But her constant avoidance of me was really beginning to trouble me. One little visit would put my mind at ease, and I could tell her about what was going on with her great-grandmother.

●●●

The plan was for Gwen and me to get on the road Friday morning, drive to Mother's house, and spend the weekend. I sent Beatrice a plane ticket, so she would have no excuse not to be there. Her plane would land at four o'clock Friday afternoon. My offer to pick her up from the airport was quickly declined. She insisted on catching a taxi to Mother Clara's house.

Since I was delighted she was coming, I didn't complain. All of the Kendall sisters together was something that hadn't happened in over thirty years.

Even though Beatrice and I spoke from time to time, I could tell she didn't trust me. As children, the only time we began to form a bond, our mother tore her away from us, and we never saw her again. She didn't even tell us that our mother had passed years ago. I would have thought my mother would have wanted her funeral to be where she had grown up and where her family was. But like always, when dealing with Ruth Ann, I had been wrong. She had given Bea strict instructions on how to handle her burial arrangements. A part of me had always been resentful of the relationship Bea had with our mother.

We never had the opportunity to get as close to her or to know her the way Bea had. There was this deep seed of abandonment Gwen and I had felt from our mother. But it was nothing like the pain Mother Clara had caused. Gwen had not forgiven our mother nor Mother Clara, and honestly, I had not either. Forgiveness was one thing we were not taught growing up and hadn't come to terms with as adults.

•••

Before I went to pick Gwen up to start our journey to Mother's house, I needed to ease my anxiety by seeing my daughter. I had a strong gut feeling something was amiss, and my gut never lied to me. I arrived at her apartment at ten that morning, aware she did not leave for work until noon. I also knew her boyfriend would be at work during this time, and I would have more of an opportunity to candidly speak with her. We had always been so close until she moved out. I missed her so much, but I knew she was grown now and had to live her own life. As a mother, however, I never stopped worrying about my child.

Ashley Homes Apartment Complex personified college living beyond the boundaries of campus. The trees came alive and danced to their own collegiate songs as the wind stirred around them. I spotted my daughter's silver Honda and slowly pulled into the parking space beside it. Her apartment was on the ground floor. For that, I was thankful since I had had another dizzy spell this morning while getting dressed.

As usual, Harold had not returned home yet from his second family. I was left alone in the house, trying to steady myself to finish putting my clothes on.

I put the thoughts of my health on the backburner for the moment to concentrate on Mia. My intuition that everything was not great, like Mia always proclaimed, grew more intense as I got closer to her door.

I knocked on the door twice before I heard any movement.

"Who is it?" Mia asked.

"Your mother."

It took her at least a minute to open the door. I began wondering if she was going to let me in. She cracked the door, with the chains still on the locks, and peered out as if I was a stranger.

"Uh, Mom, what are you doing here?"

"Mia, let me in," I said, my frustration written all over my face.

"I was just about to leave," Mia lied. Dark sunglasses covered her eyes as if she was about to head out the door. But the white cotton robe draped around her made it appear as if she had just gotten out of the shower.

"So, you were going out in your robe?" I asked, sounding sarcastic. "I am going to say this one more time; let me in." I gently pushed on the door to let her know I was serious.

"Okay, okay, Mom, just wait," Mia huffed. She closed the door and unhooked the chain so that she could open it.

I walked through the doorway, which lead straight into the living room, and took a seat on her black leather couch. Mia sat down across from me in the matching recliner. Her long hair weave was matted in the back and needed to be taken out. The few curls that were still there looked dry, as if they were going to break off immediately. Mia had always prided herself on her appearance. Seeing her like this deepened my feeling that something was wrong.

"Please remove your sunglasses," I instructed in the motherly tone I had used with Mia most of her life. It was loving but letting her know I meant business.

"Momma, please," Mia begged.

"Mia, don't play with me. I am still your mother."

Mia slowly removed the sunglasses from her face. When I saw the purplish-black mark that circled her eye, I wanted to cry and curse.

"Baby, did he do this to you?" I asked, fighting my nerves.

"Mom, it was just an accident." Mia turned away from me and stared at the floor.

Being in the same situation for many years, I knew not to fuss and get overdramatic right away. That was not what Mia needed. She needed to know I loved her. Even though it was hard for me to do, I took a deep breath, stood, and walked over to Mia. I bent down and put my arms around my only child.

She allowed me to hold her for a few seconds and then pulled away. "Mom, it's not what you think. He loves me, and I love him."

The mother in me couldn't hold it in any longer. "Baby, a man that hits you does not love you."

Mia laughed, "That's saying a lot coming from you."

"What are you trying to say, girl?" I took two steps back and stared at my daughter, daring her to continue with her thoughts.

"Nothing, Mom," Mia mumbled. "I'm just trying to live my life, that's all. He loves me, and we have problems. But we can work through them. Isn't that what you taught me?"

I didn't have enough time to let my daughter know how I felt about her and her boyfriend fighting. And with the smart comment she had just made, I wasn't even sure she would hear me out. Was all this my own fault?

"Mia, I am on my way to visit Mother Clara, but we will finish this when I get back," I said, walking toward the door. "I love you."

"I love you, too, Mom."

As I walked to my car, I stopped and glanced back at Mia's apartment. She had already gone inside and closed the door. I said a quick prayer, asking God to protect my only child.

Chapter 22

Gwen

Even though seeing Mother Clara was the last thing on my mind, I knew I couldn't get out of going to Timmonsville with Rina. As Rina glided onto Interstate 26, beginning our two-hour journey to Mother's house, memories began to suffocate me. I was used to breathing a little heavier than most people. As I remembered all the beatings and abuse, it felt like I was being submerged in water, struggling to be free.

"You okay?" Rina asked. She glanced at me, noticing I was trying to catch my breath.

I held my chest, trying to slowly breathe in and out like the doctor had instructed me to do the last time I went to the emergency room for an anxiety attack.

"Ri Ri, I just don't think I can do this," I said, still clutching my chest.

"Okay, Sis, just settle down. Take deep breaths, in and out."

I glanced at Rina and thought about all the times she had spoken these same words to me as a child. All the many times she had calmed me down and repeated to me over and over that everything would be all right. I believed her since she made sure to do whatever it took to make things better for me. She had only missed one night that she knew of. The only other time she was not there I never told her about. I did not tell anyone. After all these years, I felt like I was still missing a piece of me.

Her voice soothed me, and I was finally able to collect myself. "There is nothing good at that house, Rina," I said, sounding like my twelve-year-old self.

"Gwen, you ever thought about the fact that we are who we are today because of that house?"

"What do you mean?"

"We are how we were raised. That house still has a hold on us to an extent."

"Well, it didn't seem to affect you. You have accomplished so much and have a loving husband, great career, and daughter despite the awful way we were bought up. You are nothing like we were raised."

"It's not as perfect as it seems," Rina mumbled.

"Huh?" I asked, confused. Rina had never said anything negative about her marriage. I always prayed that God would send me someone as good as my brother-in-law, Harold.

"Never mind."

We rode in silence for another hour, listening to a mixture of Jill Scott, Mary J. Blige, and Raheem Devaughn from a Sirius satellite station. I had so many thoughts swirling around in my head that it was impossible for me to stay quiet any longer.

"Rina, how can you go down there every few months even after what we went through?"

"I don't think about it."

"Well, why did you stop?" I asked.

"I just did," Rina simply replied.

For the first time in months, I stared at my sister. Rina drove me to work every day since my car had been repossessed, and I barely looked at her. I noticed she was more gray than usual and had small dark bags under her eyes. I was so used to her always being there for me that I had not picked up on the fact she was looking older and even losing weight.

"Sis, have you been sick recently?" I asked, observing that her wedding ring was now hanging loosely from her ring finger. Guilt replaced my anxiety as I realized I had paid so little attention to the changes in my sister's appearance. I was so focused on my own issues that I hadn't even recognized my sister might be going through some things as well.

"Don't worry about me. It's just hot flashes now and then. I think I'm going through the change," Rina replied, acting nonchalant.

"Sis, you are almost fifty. Shouldn't you have gone through the change years ago?" I laughed.

Rina took her eyes off the road long enough to look at me. "Everyone is different. Now hush about that. I told you I'm fine."

Taking her word for it, I left that conversation alone only to go back to the previous one.

"Why don't we ever talk about what happened when we were young?" Years and years of horrible dreams harassed me until I was well into my thirties. Now at forty-six, the dreams were not as consistent. But some nights, I stayed up just to make sure they didn't come back. There were times when I was terrified to go to sleep because I did not want to relive what happened to me. Once, I even thought about therapy. But like most black people I knew, we were told just to pray about it and let God handle it.

"I never thought you wanted to."

"Sometimes I do, and sometimes I don't. But going back to this house that I haven't been to in over twenty years…Well, I don't know," I said, gazing out of the window again.

"Beatrice should be there when we arrive," ClaRina informed me.

I wasn't sure if she was trying to change the subject or just prepare me for the wreck that was our other sister. Granted, I didn't really know her. But what I did know of her, I didn't like.

"Ugh, make sure you hide your wallet." I folded my arms over my chest like I used to do when I was a little girl.

"Don't be like that! She is your sister!"

"Half," I replied.

"It doesn't matter. She is the same as you and me," Rina reminded me. Of course, Rina and I were half-sisters, too. But in my heart and mind, it did not feel like that. Growing up, she was all I had. And truth be told, except for my kids, she was still all I had.

"I just don't like her, Rina," I whined. "We both know she on that shit, and I would rather not spend my weekend with a crackhead, sister or not."

"Gwen, that was just mean. This is the time to get to know her, and neither one of us has room to judge."

Rina was right in some aspect. But to be honest, I had no desire to get to know my "other" sister. Rina and Bea talked from time to time, but I never reached out to her, and, in return, she did the same. When we were little, she thought she was better than us because she lived in New York with our mother and not having to go through the things we did. In my mind, she was better, and I hated her for that.

"I'm not making any promises," I replied, and turned the music up to ensure the conversation was done.

Chapter 23

Beatrice

The last time I had been down South with my mother, I was ten, and she was telling me not to ever trust "these" people. Indeed, the people she referred to happened to be my family, but I didn't know them; therefore, I didn't trust them. To be honest, I didn't have any faith in anyone. All my life, people showed me over and over that I could not count on anyone. I used them for what I could. Then when I was done, I threw them away. I was at the end of my rope, and just like I had done with everyone else, I would use my dying grandmother and her house for as long as I could.

Once I arrived at the airport, I called a taxi to take me to the address Rina had texted me. I hadn't been there since I was a kid. There was no way I could have remembered any street names or landmarks. Riding through the barely paved streets and looking at all the fields was like traveling back in time. It was as if time skipped over this ancient town and allowed it to just stay in the good ole days. But I could not see anything good about those days or this hick country ass town.

"Oh, God, are you serious?" I asked out loud. I watched an elderly white man, dressed in overalls with a straw hat covering his head, riding down the street on a tractor.

"First time down South, young lady?" My taxi driver's deep Southern drawl made it difficult to even piece together what he was saying. Just like the tractor driver, he looked as if he was stuck in the fifties, too. His bald head made a glare on the windshield and caused me not to look directly in front of me.

"I'm sorry, what was that?" I asked, leaning forward in the backseat, hoping this would help me understand my driver better.

"Ever been here before? I can tell by yo' accent you from up North," he replied. This time, a little slower.

"It's been a very long time. It looks like it did back when I was a child."

"Well, if you need somebody to show you 'round, I'm available. Name is Ed," he said, winking at me through his rearview mirror. All I could think about was how badly he could use some Vaseline on his crusty white lips.

"No, thanks. I'm sure you need all your little taxi money," I replied, turning my nose up at Ed. I didn't care if I offended him or not, but I was sure that I was well out of his league. Even without a place to live, I could do a lot better than him.

"Excuse me, miss lady." Ed chuckled and focused back on the road.

Thankful for the silence, I continued to gaze out of the window. I intended to stay long enough to see what the old woman had left me and then get back to New York as fast as I could. My home was up North, and even though I was running from Damon, I had to go back soon. I definitely could not stay down here in this slow-paced, ancient, backwoods place.

"We are here," Ed announced, pulling into Mother Clara's driveway. The rundown white shack was a remnant of the house from the television show *Little House on the Prairie.*

"Are you sure this is the correct address?" I questioned. There was no way I was going to stay at this dump for even a few days. My apartment may not have been a mansion, but it was better than this rundown, dilapidated house that should have been condemned years ago.

Mother Clara's yard resembled an old black and white photograph taken in the 1920s. The driveway was merely dirt and rocks. Parked on the right side of the house was a rusted black pickup truck. The once green grass was now standing tall and brown, surrounding the house and vehicle like it was the owner. A few yards from the house stood a small building that looked as if it could have once been a shed or storage unit. It was partially burned down and seemed as if the remaining part that was still barely standing would completely crumble to the ground at any moment.

I slowly climbed out of Ed's taxi and grabbed my suitcase.

"Just in case ya change ya mind." Ed handed me a piece of paper with his phone number written on it.

Standing in Mother Clara's yard, I began to regret my decision to come down here. What did I care what the old woman had to tell me or had for me? I stood in the driveway for at least ten minutes. When I suddenly looked up, a tall, slender woman stood in the open doorway of my grandmother's house. I must have been in a complete daze because I didn't even realize when the door had opened. The lady motioned for me to come toward her. As if still in a trance, I obeyed.

The closer I got to her, the more my body relaxed, and I felt a sudden calmness. As I approached the screen door, she opened it, smiled, and instructed me to come in.

"You must be, Beatrice," she said, in a knowing tone, reaching her hand out for me to shake. I sat my suitcase down in the entryway and quickly shook her hand.

"Yes, I am," I responded. "And you are?"

"I'm Ms. Clara's hospice nurse, Vanessa," she smiled, showing a beautiful set of crisp white teeth.

Vanessa's light brown hair fell in loose curls halfway down her back and dropped over her shoulders as she reached down to retrieve a napkin that had fallen to the floor.

"I take care of Ms. Clara most of the day now," she said, staring at me as if she was waiting for me to say more than I already had.

Her hazel eyes curiously traveled from my head to my feet. I guess she was trying to do the same thing I was. Trying to feel me out. "She has been waiting for you girls to get here."

"How is she?" I asked. Usually, I wouldn't fake concern, but something told me that Vanessa wasn't going to let me be until I seemed as if I cared.

"It's been a good day." Vanessa smiled again. "She is sleeping right now but should be up soon." Her Southern accent twirled upon my ears and was not annoying like Ed's had been a few minutes earlier.

"She told me to show you to your room and let you get settled. It's straight down the hall, second room on your left."

I picked up my suitcase and followed her down the hall toward the room I would be staying in for the next few days. At least I hoped it would be no longer than that before the old woman took her final breath.

Chapter 24

ClaRina

"I'm glad y'all were able to make it." Vanessa smiled at me. I had talked to her several times on the phone, but this was the first time meeting her in person.

As Gwen, Beatrice, and I piled into Mother Clara's room, an air of tension and uncertainty circled her bed along with us. Silence was the main visitor now as we looked upon Mother Clara, not knowing what to expect. We were strangers in our hearts but family through our blood.

Mother Clara was resting in a wide metal hospital bed that looked as if it was not strong enough to hold her. Monitors and an IV (intravenous), standing beside the bed, were connected to her, sustaining what little life she had left. The bed took up most of the space in the miniature room; therefore, there was only one other chair to sit in—Mother Clara's favorite wooden rocking chair. I was surprised to see the ancient chair was still intact. Above Mother's head, mounted on the plain wall, was a picture of Grandpa Henry. Once I spotted the photograph of that repulsive and vile man, a bitter chill ran through my body. I quickly turned my attention to my sister just to stop the memories from overtaking me.

Beatrice avoided my glances and kept her eyes locked on the picture of Grandpa Henry. Her petite frame was covered in an oversized faded red T-shirt and baggy black faded jeans. Her medium length hair that was in need of a good wash and conditioning was brushed back in a ponytail. And her dusty Converse sneakers were one step away from needing to be tossed in the trash. From what I had known, Beatrice had always been small. But the weight she was now made me wonder just how bad off she really was.

When Gwen and I arrived at the house, Bea was already there. She did not say more than two words to us. After the first initial glance, she didn't even look at us anymore.

I tried to strike up a conversation with her but to no avail. Gwen and Bea glanced at each other as if they were strangers and meeting for the first time. In all honesty, even though we were all sisters, we didn't know one another.

"Your grandmother is very weak but was persistent about talking to you girls," Vanessa informed us while straightening Mother's pillows.

Mother Clara laid in her bed as still as the day Grandfather Henry had died. If it weren't for the blinking of her eyes every few seconds and the slight rise and fall of her chest, I would have sworn she was already six feet under. Draped in a white hospital gown, she was half the size of the woman who raised us. Her small silver afro was neatly packed on top of her head, but the intense scowl upon her face was still present, a reminder of my childhood.

"Ms. Clara," Vanessa whispered to Mother. Mother Clara stared straight ahead as if she was under a spell or watching a TV show that had her full attention. However, there was no television in her room, so I questioned if she was still completely in her right mind.

"Ms. Clara, look who is here to see you," Vanessa repeated Mother's name louder this time. Suddenly, Mother snapped out of her daze. Her eyes shifted from me to Gwen to Bea.

She motioned for Vanessa to lift her into a better sitting position. Her nurse did as she was instructed and took the bed remote to lift the top of Mother's bed. Mother raised her hand to let Vanessa know to stop, and she was comfortable enough.

Mother cleared her voice. "Thank y'all for coming."

My thoughts went back to when we were children. At that second, it hit me that I had never heard the words thank you come from Mother Clara's mouth.

Even when I had come to help her clean before her illness took a turn for the worst, she never said those two simple words expressing gratitude. The most she said, which led me to believe she was grateful, was that she was glad to see me.

Silence took over as we all waited for Mother to speak again. I turned to look at Vanessa, checking the monitors Mother was hooked up to.

"Is everything okay?" I asked, noticing that Mother had closed her eyes just that quickly. Vanessa glanced down at Mother and then back at the monitors.

"I think that's all she'll be able to handle for today, ladies," Vanessa said, addressing us.

For a second, we all stood there, not knowing what to do next. Since the plan was to talk to Mother as soon as we got there, we didn't realize we would have to wait another day to hear why she wanted all of us to visit so badly.

"You ladies can get settled while I make Ms. Clara more comfortable."

Taking that as our cue to leave, Gwen and Beatrice followed me out of Mother's room.

"Bea, have you gotten your luggage placed in one of the rooms?"

"Yeah, I'm in the backroom," Beatrice responded, heading to her room. Again, she did not look at Gwen or me.

"Well, are you hungry? You want to grab something with Gwen and me? It's still early, and I know I'm starving."

"Nah, I'm good," Bea said, walking into her room and closing the door behind her.

"This is going to be a long weekend, Sis. Bet if you had some drugs, her ass would have went," Gwen chuckled, and rolled her eyes at Bea's closed door.

I usually tried to see the silver lining in all situations, but as I looked at Gwen, then down the hall at the door Beatrice had just slammed, I couldn't come up with anything positive at this moment.

Chapter 25

Beatrice

I had hoped the old lady would get to the point of why we were all called to see her as soon as we got there. Unfortunately, she did not. Now I was sitting in this mothball smelling room, trying to sleep. Even though it was early evening, I thought to try and get some rest since I was feening and had no way to get what I needed right now. I was sick of this town, house, room, and old lady already, and I had just gotten here. Looking around this shack, if the bitty had any money, it probably was not a lot. I was starting to believe my visit would be worthless.

There has to be more to it than what meets the eye, I thought, surveying my surroundings. In the corner of this almost bare room was a dresser that seemed as old as I was. At one time, it looked as if it might have been cherrywood. But over the years, most of the paint had been chipped away. I walked over to the dresser and struggled to pull the top drawer open. Once I finally got inside of it, I saw there was an antique rectangular-shaped brass jewelry box.

"Well, well, well, what do we have here," I said out loud as if someone else were standing behind me.

Maybe my trip down here would not be a total waste after all, I thought while picking the jewelry box out of the drawer and placing it on the dresser. I opened the box and saw the most elegant angel brooch I had ever laid my eyes upon. The wings of the angel were covered in diamonds that even the poorest man could see were real. Ruby stones circled the outline of the angel, and in the center of the angel's gown was a diamond larger than the others. Heart-shaped and flawless, the diamond had to be worth at least a few thousand dollars or more.

Although I knew I was alone in my room, and the door was closed, I still looked around to see if anyone was watching me before I placed the brooch in my pocket. As soon as it was safely tucked away deep in my jeans, I heard a slight knock on the door.

"Bea, you sure you don't want to come with us?" Rina asked from the other side of the door.

I hesitated for a moment. I sure was hungry, and it probably would be almost impossible to find anything to eat in this house. Maybe while I was out, I could talk to someone in the area to see if I could get something to ease my other cravings as well.

Reaching in my pocket, I retrieved the brooch. Just in case Rina and Gwen were nosy, I would leave it in my suitcase tucked down at the very bottom. That way, if someone noticed it was missing, even though I highly doubted it being that Mother Clara and Vanessa were the only other two people here, no one would be able to find it on me.

I opened the door and was face to face with both Rina and Gwen.

"Yeah, all right," I said, closing the door behind me. I might as well milk everyone for everything I could while I was down here.

•••

I sat in the back of Rina's BMW and listened to the conversation between her and Gwen. It was obvious they were extremely close and talked daily. They even lived only twenty minutes from one another. Their friendship made me resent that I had no one growing up, and most of my time growing up was spent alone. We may be sisters and share the same blood, but we were definitely not the same.

"So, how is your job going, Bea? You still with the same company?" Rina asked, attempting to include me in her and Gwen's chat.

"Yeah."

There was an awkward silence as if Rina expected me to elaborate, but I did not feel the need. I didn't have a stellar career helping people like she did. I also was sure I didn't make as much money as Gwen did at the post office. No reason for me to even talk about my insignificant job.

"You dating anyone? Got a boo up there in New York?" Rina again tried to get me to talk to her.

I glanced at her suspiciously and wondered why she wanted to know my personal business. We spoke from time to time, but our talks never got too deep. She just checked in to see if I was still alive.

I sighed. "Nah, I don't."

Finally, Rina took the hint and turned up the radio. Now that she and Gwen were being drowned out by Erykah Badu crooning about her next lifetime, I relaxed in my seat and tried to figure out how I could get more money before going back up North. I turned to my right and saw Rina's Dooney & Burke purse sitting on the floor under the passenger side seat. It was partially open, and her wallet was sitting right on top.

Rina and Gwen were grooving to the music and not paying me any attention. I glanced at the wallet again and tried to figure out how I could get it without drawing attention to myself. Suddenly, as if Gwen was reading my mind, she turned the radio down.

"Sis, do you have any gum in your purse?"

"Yeah, I think so. Look in there to see." Rina nodded to the back where her purse was placed.

Gwen turned around to retrieve the purse and smirked at me.

I balled my fists up and fought the urge to punch Gwen in her fat ass mouth. Instead, I just gazed out of the window and remembered the brooch I had hidden in my suitcase. That bitch had no idea it was in my possession, and I would be long gone before anyone found out.

Chapter 26

Gwen

I despised being around Beatrice when she was little and even more now that she was here with us. It was true that she was younger than me. But just looking at the two of us side by side, anyone would think she was at least ten years older. Her stringy, greasy black hair that stopped at her shoulders and baggy clothes showed she didn't have a pot to piss in. However, she acted as if she had more than Rina and me. My point was proven that she had absolutely nothing when I caught her eyeing Rina's purse out of my front seat mirror. I started to bust her little thieving ass, but Rina repeatedly expressed how much she wanted Bea and me to get along, at least for the weekend. Therefore, instead of outing the rouge, I simply made sure she didn't take anything from Rina.

Since there were no decent restaurants in the small town where we grew up, we had driven about twenty-five minutes to the next closest city of Florence. Dinner at Clyburn's Steakhouse always helped brighten my dismal moods, considering it was one of my favorite restaurants. I had just finished the last little bit of my chicken parmesan and was already thinking about the mouth-watering chocolate cake I was planning to order for dessert. Even though I was sitting across from Beatrice, who I could not stand, the food more than made up for my displeasure.

"So, what do you think the old lady wants to talk to us about?" Bea asked, stuffing a fork full of garlic mashed potatoes into her mouth. Another indication she did not have shit was that Rina had offered to take care of the bill, and Beatrice happily accepted.

I watched her order the biggest steak on the menu with a side of everything from salad to corn to the mashed potatoes she was currently chomping on like this was her first meal and last supper all wrapped up in one.

It seemed quite comical for her to want to talk now when Rina had done her best to start a conversation with her in the car. "Well, we are not sure what our grandmother wants, Beatrice," I said in the most sarcastic tone I could give her.

Bea smirked while staring at my now empty plate. "You probably should have ordered a salad before you can't fit in the room when she wants to talk to us."

"Hold on one minute," I started. I put my fork down and looked at this raggedy bitch who had the audacity to talk about my looks when she appeared a dime away from being homeless.

"Wait, y'all, just wait," Rina pleaded, cutting me off right before I was about to dig into Beatrice and let her know she had better watch her mouth when speaking to me.

"Do you both realize that you're sisters?" Rina asked. "You both have the same blood flowing through each of you, and you behave like strangers."

"That's because we are," I mumbled underneath my breath.

"And that needs to change, right here and right now," Rina announced, obviously hearing what I had said.

At this point, I had nothing left to say, and neither did Beatrice, who was still eating her mashed potatoes as if Rina was only talking to me.

"We are all sisters and need to get to know one another," Rina said in the tone she used to always calm me down. "And we all had terrible childhoods."

"Yeah, everyone but Beatrice," I inserted. "She has no idea what we went through."

"Bitch, you don't know what I been through!" Beatrice shouted, tossing her fork on the table. "You didn't have to sit in the closet and wait for the beatings to stop. You didn't have to feed and raise yourself. You don't know what it was like for me, so I would suggest you keep your fat ass mouth shut."

"I would rather be fat than to look like a crackhead!" I screamed at Beatrice. I was about to go in more until I saw our waitress rushing toward our table.

"Can you ladies please keep it down?" she asked, waving her menu in a downward motion. The slender blonde lady stood at the table a minute too long, just staring at us. Before I had a chance to respond, Rina stepped in.

"We apologize. Please bring us the check, and we will leave shortly," Rina said, giving the waitress her best smile. Her calm nature worked once again as the lanky blonde thanked her and turned around to go get our check.

"That was unnecessary," Rina hissed. "Gwen, we don't know what Bea has been through. And, Bea, that was uncalled for to insult Gwen. We are sisters!"

A cloud of guilt covered me as I let Rina's words sink in. Although I hated how Beatrice said it, she was right. I didn't know what she went through in New York with Ruth Ann. Growing up, I always thought she had it better than us, but maybe all this time, I was wrong. Maybe she had it rough, too.

"I'm sorry, Beatrice. Because of everything we went through, we always assumed you and Ruth Ann were living the good life in New York."

"The only reason I liked coming down here when I was little was because I was guaranteed to eat," she laughed.

The waitress returned to the table. Once Rina paid the bill for all three of us, we headed back to Timmonsville.

On the ride home, I learned a little more about Beatrice. She was more talkative and just a bit more open compared to the ride to the restaurant. Not sure if that was because of the cocktails we had at dinner, but it helped me understand her a tad better. Even though I could tell she was still guarded, the fact that she even chatted a little made my dislike for her slightly fade.

Like Rina said, we were sisters, and Mother Clara brought us together for a reason. Now, all we needed to do was find out why she had us come to Timmonsville one more time.

Chapter 27

ClaRina

"Hello, hello," I repeated, confused about what had just happened. Of all these years, she had never been this bold to answer my husband's phone. No matter if she was his mistress and had kids together, he was my husband by law. And law won every time.

I punched the numbers on my phone so hard that I almost broke a nail, trying to dial Harold's number again. Whether it be him or her, whoever answered his cell phone was about to get blasted. The phone continued to ring and then went to his voicemail. At first, I wasn't going to leave a message. But I had been more than fair in this entire arrangement; I didn't deserve to be disrespected even more than I already was. In all honesty, the situation between myself, Harold, and his mistress was more like a decree than a simple arrangement. Harold had always worked late nights, therefore I never suspected he was cheating at all. When we hit the fifteen-year mark in our marriage it was cause for a great celebration since most of the married couples I knew did not make it that long. But here we were, celebrating ten years of good and bad moments. We weren't the college kids all over each other anymore, but all couples went through a drought where they barely touched each other—at least that's what I thought. But all my thoughts and hopes for another happy fifteen years changed once he told me about his mistress. I remember the conversation like it was yesterday as we sat at dinner reminiscing about our years together.

Harold cleared his throat. "Rina, there is something I need to tell you."

I smiled at him, waiting to hear what he had to say.

"I have a baby on the way."

"Huh?" I asked. I laughed at the obvious joke that he was trying to play on me.

"I'm not joking. I have a baby on the way." Harold loosened his tie and glanced around the restaurant, obviously in hopes that I wouldn't cause a scene.

Aware of our surroundings, I calmed myself down. "Harold, keep talking," I demanded.

"We can talk about it at home." He raised his hand and beckoned the waiter over to our table.

Once we got in the car, I recall screaming, cursing, and crying. After unleashing all my emotions and rage toward my husband of ten years, Harold made his decree.

"Rina, I still love you and want our marriage. We live a lavish life and I know you do not wish to give that up. I will handle this situation. Just trust me. You will not leave me though. Think about our daughter. Mia is only five years old and needs both of us."

Even now those words floated around in my head. And Harold was right, I didn't leave him. I stayed and allowed him to leave every Friday to be with his other family. Harold's voicemail caught my attention and pulled me from the memories of our past.

"Harold, call me back as soon as you get this. I don't know what's going on, but I do not appreciate that woman answering your phone," I whispered into the phone just in case someone was listening at my bedroom door. We were waiting around for Vanessa to tell us when we could go in and talk to Mother Clara. The last update she had given us was an hour ago, informing us that Mother had to take her medicine and be given some time for it to work throughout her system.

I turned to walk toward my bed and started to feel lightheaded. My head began to swim, and I felt faint from another dizzy spell. They were getting worse by the day.

Harold, Mia, and Mother Clara were causing me more stress than I cared to admit, and it was quickly affecting my daily health. I sat down on the bed and tried to calmly breathe in and out, so the room would stop spinning. I could not delay it any longer. As soon as I returned home, I would go see my doctor.

I closed my eyes and heard a gentle knock on the door before it opened.

"Rina, the nurse said Mother could see us now," Gwen said, sticking her head in the door. She rushed in and over to the bed as soon as she saw that I was trying to catch my breath.

"You okay? What's wrong?" Gwen rubbed my back, trying to calm me down.

I took another deep breath. "Yeah, just another dizzy spell. You know your sister is not as young as she used to be." I sought to make light of the situation, so the worried look covering Gwen's face would disappear. Even when I was sick, I was still concerned about how my baby sister felt.

Seeing that I was not making a big deal of my health seemed to relax Gwen. She stood up from the bed. "You ready to get this thing started?"

"As ready as I will ever be."

I followed Gwen out of my room and into Mother Clara's room.

Hooked up to more tubes than she was the day before, we all could see that death was hovering over her, waiting for the right time to take Mother Clara. The fact that she could still talk and was in her right mind was amazing in itself.

Beatrice was already in the room, sitting in Mother's rocking chair and staring up at the picture on the wall like she had done yesterday. It was as if she did everything possible to avoid looking directly at Mother Clara. She didn't acknowledge we had entered the room. Instead, she continued to gaze at the portrait.

Mother coughed, causing Vanessa to stop pressing buttons on her oxygen machine and rush toward the bed to give her a drink of water. She grabbed the remote, lifting the head of the bed so that Mother would be in a better sitting position.

Mother Clara looked at Gwen, Beatrice, and me for a moment as if she knew us but was trying to figure out who we were at the same time.

"My grandmother was a slave," she started. Her voice was low, coarse, and I strained to hear her. I inched closer to the bed so that I wouldn't miss a word.

"She worked in the fields from the time the sun rose until it set, and then she went back to the slave quarters to take care of my father and the rest of her kids."

Mother Clara coughed. On cue, Vanessa brought the cup of water to give her another drink. For the first time since she had arrived at the house, Beatrice looked at Mother.

"When my father was about twelve years old, he was taken from my grandmother. No warning, no time to say goodbye, they just took him away. So, because of that, the slaves could not show their children any love. They had to be raised strong with no emotions because they never knew when they would be taken from them. My dad raised me the same way. In return, I raised you two the only way I knew," Mother said, looking at Gwen and me. "I loved all three of you, and the only way I knew to show that was to make sure you could take care of yourselves and stand up to everything you would have to deal with just because you are black."

The room fell silent again as Mother rested her head on her pillow. "Do you need to rest, Mrs. Clara?" her nurse asked.

Mother waited a few seconds and replied, "Yes."

At her request, we all piled out of Mother's room. Before we made it into the hallway, Mother began to speak again.

"Beatrice, I would like to see you alone after my nap."

Beatrice nodded her head and turned to me. I shrugged my shoulders and continued out of Mother's room. I never expected Mother to tell us what she had just expressed.

All the years of abuse, I believed she hated Gwen and me. I honestly thought she loathed us and felt like it was a burden on her to raise us. And because of the love that I did not get as a child, I became an overbearing mother.

Never once did I even think that maybe she didn't even know how to show love. Because of the mistreatment when I was younger, I vowed to always show Mia that she was loved more than anything in the world.

My thoughts went to my only daughter and the abuse she was now dealing with. I hurried back to my room so that I could give Mia a call. The image of her black eye was branded in my head. I couldn't shake the familiar feeling I was having. She was following in my footsteps, and I could not blame anyone but myself. I constantly hid black eyes and bruises when Mia was a child. I put up with the abuse for years. I didn't want that for her. I was not going to allow her to travel the same road I had. I would give my last breath before I saw her walk a day in the same shoes my grandmother, my mom, and I had been in.

The phone rang four times, and Mia's voicemail picked up. I left a quick message on her voicemail and hoped my daughter was somewhere safe.

Chapter 28

Beatrice

I had something of value, and now I yearned to leave. Honestly, I did not care what my so-called grandmother wanted to tell me unless she was going to leave me money or another piece of her expensive jewelry. Even though she had not outright given me the brooch, I felt that it was more than owed to me. A lot was owed to me. I did not grow up living with the old bitty, having a roof over my head, and food to eat every day. There was even a time when I was five that I vaguely remembered my mom and me being homeless for a few months. My mind traveled back to the humid nights, trying to find just a little bit of shelter and the crisp mornings that followed. When I heard a sudden knock on my bedroom door, I was snapped out of my memories.

"Come in."

Vanessa popped her head in and smiled, "Ms. Clara will see you now."

As I followed her down the hall toward Mother Clara's room, I breathed in her scent. The smell of fresh flowers and shampoo tickled my nose and made me pay more attention to Vanessa, if that was possible. I had a hard time ignoring just how beautiful and calming her aura was. We walked into Mother Clara's room. For once, she was already sitting up, eyes slightly open, and breathing deeply. The only noise coming from the room was the beeping monitors that she was attached to.

I sat down in the chair that had somewhat officially become mine and stared at the picture on the wall.

"I know you don't know me," Mother Clara began, "for reasons that had nothing to do with you. Our time together was limited."

As she continued to talk, I didn't take my eyes off the picture. The framed black and white photograph of an older man with a clean-shaven face completely captured my attention. The stranger in the picture wore a hat and a button-down shirt. I couldn't tell what color the hat or shirt was since the picture wasn't in color. The man in the photograph did not have a smile nor a frown on his face. It was more like a grimace. Like he had just finished telling his kids what to do, and someone made him take a picture right after the orders. I stared at the picture because, for one, I didn't want to look at this old lady I didn't know, and two, I was more intrigued by who the man was in the picture. What was his story, and why was his picture the only one in the room?

"The man in the picture was your Grandpa Henry, my husband," Mother Clara stated as if to read my mind.

Finally, her words caught my attention and caused me to look at her. I had heard the stories of how he died, but nothing was ever confirmed. After the night my mom had left this house, she never talked about her family or anyone from here again. The only thing she ever said about her family was not to ever trust them.

"He was a hideous man; far more awful than the stories you must have heard of me," Mother Clara continued. "No matter what you do, never let a man put his hands on you. And if he does, you do whatever you need to do to protect yourself."

I was interested now and locked into what she was saying. So many nights, I had fought Ricky and my ex-husband, Gregg who started out as my first dealer, and another ex-boyfriend after him. And now that I thought about it, every relationship I had even been in had either been physically, emotionally, or verbally abusive. It was normal for me.

I had seen my mother and Ray fight my entire childhood until that day when I heard the gunshots in the living room. Although I knew it was wrong for a man to hit me, it just was not out of the ordinary for it to happen.

"Beatrice, you may have heard the rumors about how my husband died, but I can tell you the truth. I killed him, and I would do it all over again."

I was caught off guard by Mother Clara's admission and stared at her. I wasn't sure if she expected me to respond, but I was speechless.

"If a man is bold enough to put his hands on you, he can handle what comes next. I keep his picture up as a reminder that I survived him, and I can survive anything. And so can you."

I didn't know where Mother Clara was going with this, but I surely wasn't going to interrupt her now.

"I know you have a problem, and I can help."

For the first time, I spoke to the old woman. "Excuse me?"

She coughed and beaconed for Vanessa to give her a drink of water. I was so wrapped up in her story about my grandfather that I had completely forgotten we were not alone.

After sipping the water, Mother Clara repeated herself. "I know you have a problem. Vanessa, please, leave us alone."

Vanessa did as she was told and closed the door behind her.

"The only problem I have is the fact that I no longer want to be here. I came like you asked, and now it's time for me to leave." I stood from my chair and moved toward the door.

"Would fifty thousand dollars change your mind?"

I turned around to look again at the fragile lady staring back at me.

"I know about the brooch; you can keep that, and I will give you more."

Clearly, this woman was not only sick but delusional at this point. There was no way possible I would believe she had access to fifty thousand dollars. Just looking at the house and surroundings, I doubted she had five hundred dollars.

"Please, sit back down and let me explain," Mother Clara said.

If she had never said anything about any money, I would have been packing my bags and leaving. Not only did I want the money, but I honestly needed the money if there was, in fact, any money at all. I had nothing left, and if this old bitty were going to give me some of hers, then I would be more than willing to accept it.

I sat back down in the chair but prepared myself to jump up and leave if this conversation started going in a way I did not care for.

"I never had a good relationship with your mother. I was hard on Ruth Ann because I did not want her to make the same mistakes I had. And that pushed her away. I didn't do everything right by her, and I know that. I thought by raising her like I did, she would be a stronger person. Before she died, we talked, and I was too proud to tell her I was sorry. At the time, I didn't feel like I needed to apologize to her."

At this point, Mother Clara had my undivided attention again. I settled back in the rocking chair, waiting for her to finish.

"But she had great hopes for you. She talked about how smart you were, and she knew that you would have a wonderful life."

Before I could maintain my composure, tears began to fall from my eyes. I never knew my mom thought so highly of me. She never expressed that she even cared.

"I also know you need the money, so if you don't do this just for the money, do it for Ruth Ann," Mother Clara finished.

As if on cue, Vanessa knocked at the door.

"Come in," Mother Clara instructed.

"I would like for you to check into a rehab center here. I will give you time to think about it. You have until tomorrow."

Mother Clara closed her eyes as I got up and walked out of the room. She was right; I needed the money. The fact that my mother had talked about me to her made me feel differently. It made me want to try now. Hopefully, it wasn't too late for me to start.

Chapter 29

Gwen

As we crowded into Mother Clara's room again after her nap, my thoughts went back to Chris. I hadn't heard from him since the night I sat in the driveway of his house armed with a knife, waiting for him to come home. Now that I look back on that night, I was glad he hadn't pulled up in his driveway. I had fallen asleep in his yard. That morning, I came to my senses and left. However, that didn't stop me from reaching out to him. I called him at least ten times a day. Each time I did, it went straight to his voicemail. A part of me could not believe he had used me to get money to help his so-called girlfriend out. But then again, it was a never-ending cycle. I thought a man loved me, and like so many times before, he proved I could not be loved.

"Gwen, you good?" Rina asked, snapping me out of my trance.

"Yeah, but are you?" I questioned, focusing on my sister. I had only gotten maybe three hours of sleep the previous night. Still, Rina looked ten times worse than me. Her eyes were red and puffy, and in a matter of two days, it looked as if she had lost at least ten pounds.

"I'm fine," Rina replied and turned her attention back to Mother Clara.

Ever since the car ride, I noticed Rina was starting to look more tired and fragile. She had always been there to take care of me, so I had to make sure she was truly okay. I could not handle it if anything ever happened to her.

We all waited for Vanessa to finish checking Mother, so she could start talking. Then my eyes fell on Beatrice. I still somewhat despised her, even though we were attempting to get to know one another. She grew up with Ruth Ann and had the opportunity to experience what it was like having a mother, unlike Rina and me.

She may have suffered some things with Ruth Ann, but I still believed she had it far more easier than us. That alone made me have such a hard time bonding with her.

She sat in her chair like a statue, exactly like she had done the day before. But instead of her usual stare at Grandpa Henry's picture, she gazed at Mother Clara. She stared as if she had a secret that only she and Mother Clara knew. The obvious change in her demeanor only frustrated me more.

Vanessa gently helped Mother to an upright position in her bed and moved to the far corner of the room.

"Today, I would like to speak to Gwen," Mother said before drawing in a deep breath. As the days passed, she looked even more frail, as if death was staring and awaiting at the doorstep.

I was not excited about Mother wanting to speak to me. No matter what she said to me, no amount of apologies would absolve her of that dreadful day where she took the good out of me—when she ripped the joy from my body.

I hadn't gotten over that, and I never would. As soon as I graduated from high school, I left this horrendous house and never came back. Never returned to visit or to see how Mother Clara was doing. Over the years, my uncles had passed, and I did not go to any one of their funerals. The day Uncle Lee passed, I went out and celebrated. The best thing he could have ever done for me was die, and I was grateful, thankful to know the old man would forever burn in hell. And now it was Mother Clara's turn to get the same eternal damnation he had been condemned to.

As the room cleared out, I took the seat Bea had just abandoned. I did not intend to make this simple for Mother Clara, and she was going to hear how I felt about what she had done to me.

"Gwen, the first thing I want to say to you is that I am sorry. I am deeply sorry for what I did to you," Mother began.

I was surprised Mother Clara was leading off with apologizing. I wanted her to feel the pain she caused me, therefore, I was going to make her disclose what she did. If she were going to apologize, I would make the old woman say it. Say what she had done to me. I wanted to hold her accountable for the iniquities she had performed. I wanted her to utter every word of how she ruined me.

Before she could finish, I interrupted her. "And what was that?" I shot back. I stared at her baiting her to look me in my face and admit that she murdered the only joy I had experienced when I was a child.

"Gwen, I am sorry for killing your child."

Hearing Mother Clara say those words slowly turned my animosity into sorrow. I tucked my hands underneath my legs and rocked back and forth. Lowering my head, agonizing tears fell from my eyes.

"Why couldn't I keep my baby?" I asked, reverting to my fifteen-year-old self.

"You were just a child yourself. I didn't want it to be the only thing you could do," Mother Clara claimed.

After the abortion, Mother Clara made sure I never saw Billy again. The only bliss I had ever felt growing up, she had taken from me.

"I was wrong, and I'm sorry. Gwen, you are worth being loved, but you need to love yourself first."

I stared at Mother Clara. This was not the same woman who beat me and broke me down, or was it? The fact remained that she had still taken away the best part of me, and I would never get that back.

"You never cared about me, and you took my child!" The tears continued and my grief was now transforming back into revulsion. She had no right to kill my baby and an apology thirty years later could not make up for her sins.

"Gwen, the way I did it wasn't right, but I always loved you, I didn't show that to you and your sisters because I just didn't know how. Love was weakness." Mother Clara pleaded for me to understand. "Your mother left because of me, and you did the same. I can't justify my actions. Please forgive me."

I glared at my grandmother laying in her metal hospital bed and felt nothing but contempt. Her apologies fell on deaf ears and meant zero to me. For one slight second, I began to feel sorry for her but that feeling quickly evaded me. She deserved to die.

"I have someone I want you to talk to coming over later. Will you talk to them?" Mother asked.

I could not answer her. Instead, I just got up and walked toward the door.

"Gwen, before you leave, please, take this."

Mother Clara grabbed an envelope sitting on the table beside her bed and handed it to me. I wiped my tears and took the letter. I looked at the woman who had caused me so much pain one last time. For the first time, I didn't only just see an evil monster in a nightgown. I also saw an old lady begging to be forgiven. However, I was not going to give her what she wanted.

Chapter 30

ClaRina

Sometimes in life, our minds reject tragic memories. Not that we purposely try to forget what has occurred, but when a traumatic action takes place, the mind often goes into a protective mode and tries to erase what happened. Unfortunately, a smell or someone speaking about the incident can trigger the memory, and it will all come flooding back accompanied with more anguish and suffering than before.

"You were always the one that took care of everyone," Mother Clara said.

It was my turn in the room, and, unlike my sisters, I was not nervous about what Mother Clara wished to divulge upon me. Although I did not come to see Mother Clara as much as I used to, I did still visit her from time to time. In those moments, we talked more with each stay.

"When we are made to take care of everyone else, we often forget about ourselves. First, I want to say I am sorry."

Mother's apology caught me off guard. The comfort of this talk disappeared as I shifted in my chair. I ran my fingers through my hair and crossed my legs. All the times I had been here to clean and take care of her, she had never apologized to me—never said she was sorry, and never said she was wrong. She also never acknowledged the hurt she had caused my sisters and me, but especially me. I was speechless, and this seemed to be completely fine with Mother because she continued to talk.

"You never knew this, but you were the one I counted on. The one I knew would do anything I asked, and I could depend on you. I'm sorry for the years of hurt I caused you."

Mother began coughing, and Vanessa handed her the cup of water sitting on the nightstand. Vanessa's presence had become irrelevant now. I had even forgotten she was there.

"Vanessa, please, leave us for a few minutes. I'll be fine," Grandmother Clara instructed.

As she was told, Vanessa vacated the room, leaving only us there. Fear crept up on me as I wondered why Mother Clara had asked Vanessa to leave.

"I know what happened and why you stopped coming, Rina."

Mother Clara stared at me as if she were waiting for me to speak. But at that moment, I couldn't come up with anything even if I had wanted to. The good thing was, I didn't. I didn't want to talk, and I barely wanted to listen.

"I know," she repeated. "Baby, go to the doctor."

Now I was confused. Had someone informed Mother Clara about my dizzy spells that had started recently?

"Mother Clara, I assure you, I'm fine. It's just stress."

"When I was a young girl, I was raped. I was raped by an older cousin of mine. I never told anyone and never spoke about it. You are the first person I have ever even confessed this to.

In those days, we did not speak about things of that nature. It happened, and we prayed. It happened, and we pretended it didn't. It happened, and we forgot."

I sat up further in my chair and held back the tears; Mother continued with her story.

"Men folks did what they wanted, and it was no reason to say anything. Just deal with it and pray. I stopped going to church because I could not believe God would allow this to happen to me at such a young age. I didn't want y'all growing up with my way of thinking, so I made y'all go every Sunday. I wanted to think God had to be kinder to you girls than he had been to me."

"Mother," I said, trying to interrupt. My mind was flooded, and the pain would escape at any moment.

"I didn't know how to stop it with y'all. We don't talk about such things. Secrets and uncovered pain hurt more than anything else. What we do not acknowledge plagues us and continues to keep occurring. Come here, Rina."

I was merely moving like a robot now, being controlled by Mother Clara's voice. I slowly stood from the rocking chair and walked to the side of her bed. "Go to the doctor. I know why you stopped coming. I wasn't strong enough to stop it, and I will regret that until I leave this earth. Please, forgive me."

Finally, a cry escaped from the darkest and deepest part of my soul, traveled to my mouth, and as I let it out, Mother Clara grabbed me and held me close. This was the only time my grandmother had ever embraced me. She never comforted me as a child. Even as an adult, all the many times I had traveled to take care of her, there was not one time where she had wrapped her arms around me. At this moment, however, I felt like a child in need of love and in need of a shoulder to let all of my emotions out. And in Mother Clara's arms, I did just that.

"ClaRina, I need you to hear me and hear me well. I know why you stopped coming. I know what he did to you a few years ago."

Shocked that Mother Clara knew what took place made me stop crying. My body tensed, and I was now angrier than sad. She knew, and she didn't say anything. For a while, I made myself believe it was just a nightmare I'd had—me reliving my horrible childhood.

Not factual, but something I had dreamed about. But that day was real; that day really did happen. As the memories poured back into the front of my mind, I felt nauseous and weak.

"Why, why didn't you say anything? I came here to see you, and you never said anything," I stuttered. "You never helped me."

A few years ago, while visiting Mother Clara, Uncle Dale was there as well. I was not too concerned with him being present because growing up, he had never tried to take advantage of Gwen and me. He was just cruel and always ordered us around. However, little did I know this day would be different.

Mother Clara was resting, and like any other time I came to visit, I decided to clean up while she slept. I was in the bedroom Gwen and I used to share when Uncle Dale came in, startling me. I spoke and continued to clean up the room. Before I knew it, he had crept up behind me and used all his body weight to pin me up against the wall. I wasn't a young girl anymore, so my first instinct was to try and fight back and take him down. Unfortunately, I had underestimated his strength since he was now a lot older. He hit me with his cane, rendering me helpless, and had his way with me. It felt like déjà vu being molested in the room I had been assaulted in years ago. That day, instead of staying until Mother Clara woke up, I left and never returned until Dale was dead in his grave. He passed a few months after that incident from pneumonia complications, and that had to be one of the happiest days of my life.

"Rina, child, please, go to the doctor. Dale had been sick," Mother Clara pleaded with me.

"I know," I said. "I know he had pneumonia. I'm aware of how that bastard died."

Mother Clara cleared her voice and stared at me. Her eyes began to water up. "Go to the doctor. If you don't listen to nothing else I say, please, child, go see a doctor. He was a lot worse than what we said."

I turned to walk out of Mother's room. I refused to hear another word about Uncle Dale. He was dead in his grave, and any thoughts of him needed to be there as well.

"ClaRina, wait."

Mother handed me a sealed envelope. "I'm sorry. I am really sorry for everything that happened to you. Take care of yourself please, before it's too late."

Chapter 31

Beatrice

I was so sick of these damn bill collectors calling me. Every single day they behaved as if I did not know I owed them money. I rejected another call on my cell phone and thought about Mother Clara's proposition. For spending four weeks in a rehabilitation drug center, she would gift me fifty thousand dollars. If I had that money, all my problems would disappear. I could get another apartment back home and live well. I could pay Damon back with interest and not have to fret about him coming to get me. It would be a dream come true for me.

Mother Clara was waiting for my answer, and I did not have any more time to think about it. It was finally Sunday. If I accepted her offer, I would have to check into the center tomorrow. I was unsure why I was attempting to seem like I had a choice when I didn't. Was I really going to go back to New York without a dime to my name?

I knocked on Mother Clara's door, ready to accept what she was offering. I could do a month without drugs. I had been clean for more than a month before, so that was not a challenge. But this time, as soon as I got the money, I would be able to buy whatever I wanted. My possibilities would be endless. At the same time, I was also doing this for Ruth Ann. If nothing else, I could make her proud by checking into the center.

"Come in," Vanessa ordered.

Mother Clara was lying in bed with her eyes closed. "Do I need to come back later?" I asked.

"No, not at all," Vanessa nodded for me to have a seat by Mother Clara's bed. I could not help but notice Vanessa's sweet aroma again, filling up the room. I smiled at her and took a seat in Mother's chair. My eyes were fixed on Vanessa. Instantly, I got caught up in her beauty.

Her brown hair, which usually hung in curls, was pulled in a high ponytail on the top of her head. The way her hair was pulled back allowed me to see more of the natural beauty of her face. Noticing that I was staring, she grinned back at me before whispering Mother Clara's name to wake her.

Mother Clara slowly opened her eyes and a knowing smile settled on her face.

"I am going to take your offer," I announced. I didn't feel like hearing a lecture today or Mother Clara going on about her past. All she needed to know was that I was going to do as she wanted, to receive her money.

Mother Clara smiled again and cleared her voice, "Your mom knew that you would be great, and the least I can do for her is to try and help with that."

On cue, Vanessa walked over to Mother Clara and put the cup of water to her lips. She took a sip and closed her eyes for a second.

Thinking we were finished with our talk, I stood from the chair and proceeded to walk toward the door.

Mother Clara opened her eyes again. "Vanessa works at the rehab center part-time and will let me know if you complete the program."

"Oh, I didn't know I would have a babysitter," I said, glancing at Vanessa. She remained silent and continued to check Mother's monitors. I was insulted that she did not believe I would complete the program on my own without supervision.

Mother closed her eyes again. This time, she didn't open them as quickly. I turned to leave the room, knowing our conversation had truly come to an end.

•••

Tomorrow, I would check myself into the New Day Rehabilitation Center about thirty miles away from Timmonsville in the next small town of Bakersfield. I would have much rather been back in New York going to a facility there. But according to Mother Clara's rules, that was not an option. She wanted Vanessa there to monitor me and make sure I finished the program before giving me her money. I thought about trying to find a quick hit before going into the center, but I was limited in this country ass town. And the fact that I didn't know anyone made it damn near impossible to find something to take the edge off. I sat in my bed, trying to figure out if there was any way I could get a fix before going into rehab tomorrow. Suddenly, I recalled the taxi driver, Ed, giving me his phone number the day he dropped me off. I wondered if he knew anyone who could sell me something.

I searched around in my purse and was so glad I did not throw Ed's number away like I had planned on doing. I knew it was a long shot, but maybe he knew someone who knew someone else who could get me what I craved. I had been in rehab many times before; something was telling me it would be quite different down here in these backwoods.

"Hey, is this Ed?" I asked, not wanting to do the small talk since it was already late at night.

"Yes, ma'am, it is. And who may I ask is this?" Ed's thick accent traveled through the phone.

"This is Bea. I rode in your taxi a few days ago. The lady from up North," I said, hoping Ed would remember me.

"Ah, yes, the beautiful, Bea," he chuckled. "I'm surprised ya called—"

Before he could continue the pleasantries, I interrupted him. "Yeah, I just need a favor."

"I'm all ears, Ms. Bea," Ed cheerfully replied.

"I've had a rough day and need something to help relax me. You wouldn't by chance have any herbal remedies or medication, the ones I cannot buy in stores to help ease my mind, would you?"

"Hmmm, I think I may have something for ya."

"Do you recall where you dropped me off? If so, I will be standing outside in fifteen minutes."

"Yessum, you are at Ms. Clara's house. Be there shortly."

That was way too easy, I thought, putting on my sneakers and placing my hoodie over my head. With a bit of luck, country ass Ed had what I needed and wasn't just saying he did to see me. If he were playing in an attempt to just spend time with me, he surely would regret it.

Chapter 32

Gwen

I sat on the bed and cried. I sobbed for my baby that had been aborted. I wept for the love I never received as a child or an adult. I shed tears because men used me repeatedly, and I allowed it just to feel wanted. I bawled until I had no tears left. If I were at home, I would have eaten an entire red velvet cake and chased it with a pint of ice cream. That would have been the only thing that would have made me feel somewhat better for a moment.

I thought back to my time with Billy and how his smile used to make my days bearable. I never even got the chance to tell him about our baby. Instead of four kids, I should have had five. I loved all my kids. But every time I had gotten pregnant, it was only to try and keep their fathers. The only child who was made from pure and genuine love was the one Mother Clara killed. I felt like the little girl who cried herself to sleep night after night in this same room.

I stood from my bed and stared at myself in the mirror above the dresser. I was not oblivious to the fact that I was morbidly obese. It was clear as day to anyone who looked at me, and especially me, that I could die of a heart attack at any moment. The last time I stepped on a scale, the number 319 flashed on the display. I was humiliated, so I never got on another scale again. I decided that if I could find someone to love me, being overweight wouldn't matter.

"I'm ready to go!" I shouted out loud to no one. When I was younger, I could not escape this treacherous house. Now, it was a different story. This time, I would leave and never return. Mother Clara could rot in hell for all I cared.

I turned from the mirror and picked my suitcase up off the floor. I placed it on the bed, so I could pack the rest of my clothes and get the hell out of here.

I noticed the unopened envelope Mother Clara had given me before I left her room was sitting on the bed. I had forgotten all about the letter. I really was not interested in what was in the envelope, either. I wanted to toss it in the trash, but my curiosity got the best of me. I tore the letter open, not exactly knowing what to expect.

Gwen,

I'm not certain when you will get this letter, but I know it will be after my death. I am sure this will come as a shock to you, but there are a few things I need you to know. As I write this letter, I am dying. I am dying of cancer, and I have accepted that. What I have not come to terms with are the two holes in my heart, and one was because of you. Even though you may not have known this, I thought of you and ClaRina every single day. You two were the reason I left Timmonsville. My plan was to move and get settled and come get both of you.

But as we both know, things do not always go as we would like them to. I made a lot of mistakes, and I wish I could change them. My life at your grandmother's house was one I do not talk about. But because I want you to understand, I will. From the age of ten until I left, I was abused by your Grandpa Henry. Truth be told, he is not your real grandfather. He is not my real dad. So, I guess it made sense for him to beat me and molest me for not being his. The night before I left, he almost beat me to death, and I knew I had to go. I regret to this day leaving you and ClaRina behind. My life in New York was filled with living check to check and never having enough, and the abuse continued. I could not bring you all into that, and leaving you was no better either.

I do not expect forgiveness for my sins, but I just wanted you to know that I love you, and I always will. I know I could have done better by you and ClaRina, but I just didn't know how. Gwendolyn Marie Kendall, you will always be my heart.

Love,

Ruth Ann

Tears rolled down my face again. I never understood why my mother left me in this awful place, but now I knew. My mother did love me. My entire life, I thought my mother had left me without remorse. I thought I was never wanted. Night after night, I prayed Ruth Ann would come to rescue me from Mother Clara. Rescue me from the hell she'd left me in. I was not the best mother I could be, but I would never leave my kids. For years, my mind wouldn't allow me to comprehend how she could do this to me. Do this to us.

A sudden knock on the door interrupted my thoughts of Ruth Ann.

I wiped the tears from my face and said, "Come in."

Vanessa peeked her head in and smiled. "You have a visitor," she said softly.

"Who?" No one knew I was here in Timmonsville. I hadn't kept in touch with anyone, so I wasn't sure who would come to see me.

"I am not sure, but he is handsome," Vanessa replied, smiling again before disappearing into the hallway.

A handsome man coming to see me? Did Chris find me and was coming to apologize? I had not heard from him since that dreadful night. Maybe he was coming to make things right. Maybe for the first time, something good was going to happen for me. I hopped off the bed and looked in the dresser mirror once more to make sure my makeup was still intact.

I smiled slightly at the lady looking back at me. "Chris, I am coming."

●●●

I walked down the hall and stopped in mid stride once I heard music playing. The song froze me in place, and I was unable to take another step. Was I hearing things? I listened harder and indeed Aretha Franklin's voice belted out the lyrics to "Son of A Preacher Man." If someone was attempting to play a joke on me by listening to this song, it was definitely not humorous. I took a deep breath gathering myself and continued down the hall. Once I saw who was waiting for me in the living room, I stopped again and suddenly wished I had put on a looser shirt that hid more of my stomach rolls and bulges. It was not Chris. For a moment, I thought someone was playing a trick on me. Could it possibly be him?

The bald-headed, gray-bearded man stood in the middle of the living room and smiled. "Gwen Kendall, is that really you?"

I was speechless and could not believe my eyes. I wanted to speak. Instead, I stood there like a mute, unable to make a sound. Once again, I felt fifteen years old.

Dressed in a heather gray short sleeve shirt and black jeans, the man started toward me and stopped when he was mere inches away from me. An intoxicating fragrance rose from his body and tickled my nose. He threw his arms around me and squeezed tight. After a few seconds, he let go, looked at me, and then hugged me again. My body relaxed in his arms.

He released me. This time, I could speak. "Is it really y-you?" I stuttered. "Oh, my God! It can't really be you. You remembered the song?"

He smiled again, reached in his pocket for his cell phone and muted the song that had been on repeat, "In the flesh, pretty gal. And of course, I remembered."

"How-how did you know I was here?"

"Mrs. Clara sent for me." He grabbed my hand and led me over to the couch to have a seat.

"I can't believe it's you. It has been so long," I said, trying my best to hold back tears.

As if he could sense my feelings, he squeezed my hand. "I'm just as excited to see you; you are still so beautiful. So incredibly beautiful."

Finally, I was able to say his name. "Billy, you must be blind now. I am far from pretty." I nervously laughed, pulling my shirt down over my stomach.

Again, I wished I had chosen a better shirt. The green tank top I had on showed every fat roll I possessed. If I had only known he was coming.

Billy let go of my hand, gently placed it under my chin, lifted my head, and forced me to look at him. "You are even more gorgeous than the first time I laid eyes on you."

Even after all these years, Billy had the same effect on me as when I was younger. My Billy. I thought back to our child and the way Mother Clara made me get rid of it. I wondered if this was the reason she had invited him over.

All these years, I had kept this secret from him. I needed to let him know what I had been carrying in my heart for so long.

"Billy, I think I know why Mother Clara called you over," I began. "There is something I must tell you."

Billy stared at me, waiting for me to continue. I mustered up all the strength I had, told him about the pregnancy and how I was forced to get rid of his child.

He sat in silence, hanging on to my every word. Once I finished pouring out my heart to him, he placed his arms around me and held me. I laid my head on his chest and released everything I had buried inside of me. The night we shared came back to me and how loved I felt with him.

"Gwen, I never had kids of my own. That would have been my only biological child," Billy whispered.

I lifted my head and looked at him as a tear rolled down his cheek. I kissed his face where the tear had landed and then moved toward his lips. He wrapped his arms around me. For the next five minutes, we kissed as if we were young lovers again. We kissed away the pain of losing our child and never being able to grieve together. We caressed as if we were the only ones in the terrible house that had caused me so much hurt. We touched as if we were alone and in love.

Chapter 33

ClaRina

I was ready to leave. I had honestly had enough, and it was time for me to return to my life. I struggled to sit up in the small twin bed that had been my resting place for the last two nights. Again, I was awakened by a migraine. Even though I had gotten at least nine hours of sleep, I was fatigued. I was constantly taking pain relievers and didn't realize how much until the other day when I was totally out of a bottle, I had just bought a couple of days before. Although I did not want to admit it to Mother Clara, I was sure it was time for me to see a doctor. I did not quite understand her requests for me to make an appointment, but my symptoms now definitely warranted a visit. Last night's events came flooding back, and as much I tried, I could not hold back the tears.

My phone was on the bed beside me, vibrating. I saw Harold's name flash on the screen. As I reached for it, something stopped me. Beside my phone was the letter Mother Clara had given me last night. I was mentally and physically exhausted, but something inside me convinced me that I needed to read the letter. I grabbed the envelope and opened it with shaking hands.

ClaRina,

I know this letter will come as a surprise to you, and if you are reading this, that means the cancer has taken me away. From the first time I laid eyes on you, my beautiful firstborn, I knew that you would be a powerful woman. I wish I had played more of a part in helping you become that woman, but I know I did not. Every night, I would pray that God would watch over you and that you would watch over Gwen. I know you do not understand why I left, but I had no choice, or you all would have been burying me a lot sooner than you had to.

I was molested and abused by my stepfather, your grandfather Henry. Yes, you read that right, Grandpa Henry was not my real father, and he made me pay for that every single day. I know this is not an excuse for leaving y'all, but I had to. And the life that I went to wasn't any better. Not good enough to bring my two girls into. I know no number of apologies will make you forgive me for abandoning you and Gwen, but I want you to know I loved y'all the best I could. Love had to be taught to me and, even as I write this letter, I still don't exactly know how to truly love someone. I do know that I loved my girls, all three of y'all. I didn't tell you that I was dying because I didn't want you to grieve for a mother who was never there. I remember when I came for Henry's funeral. I wanted to talk to you and spend time with you, but I was told I could not. That's what started the fight and why I left so quickly. I know this letter will never make up for the pain I caused, but I wanted you to know I am terribly sorry and that I love you more than you will ever know.

Love,

Ruth Ann

I read my mother's words over again. Uncle Bo always told us that Ruth Ann left for us, but I never understood why. And to find out that the man I always thought was my grandfather was not my biological grandfather had left me astonished. He made me pay for my mother leaving many nights and made me hate her even more. I thought about the last time I saw Ruth Ann and the way she snatched Bea up in the middle of the night and left. Memories poured back into my head as my phone started ringing again. Harold's name appeared on my screen once more. I had not talked to him since the day I called after his mistress answered the phone.

"Hello," I answered, distracted by the thoughts of Ruth Ann.

"You need to come home," Harold said abruptly.

"What's going on, Harold?"

"Mia is in the hospital. Come home."

"Oh, no, Harold! What happened?" I asked, instantly panicking.

"Just come home," Harold growled before hanging up on me.

I dialed Harold's number back and waited for him to answer. Once his voicemail prompted me to leave a message, it was evident he wasn't going to answer or even call me back.

"Asshole!" I screamed at my phone, tossing it on the bed. Throwing my clothes in my suitcase as fast as possible, I said a quick prayer that Mia was okay. The only thing that mattered now was me getting to my daughter.

•••

We rode in complete silence on the way home. Gwen sat with a goofy smile on her face, and I already knew the reason—Billy. I had not seen Billy in forever. I must say, the years had been kind to him. He was even more handsome now than when he and Gwen used to crush on each other when they were younger. I had to do something to take my mind off my troubles, so I finally broke the quietness.

"What's the silly grin for?" I asked, already knowing the answer to my question.

Gwen glanced at me and rolled her eyes. "You already know, Rina."

"So, you and Mr. Billy had a good talk last night?"

"Oh, Rina, he is just like I remembered him but even more amazing!" Gwen exclaimed.

"So that's why you are so giddy this morning?"

Gwen blushed. "We are going to stay in touch, and he has already asked to come visit me. His wife passed a year ago, and he said he has not thought about dating again until he saw me."

"I'm glad you are happy, Sis."

"I am, but why did we leave in such a rush? What's going on?"

During my panic of trying to leave, I had failed to fill Gwen in on Mia being in the hospital.

"Harold called and told me that Mia was in the hospital. I don't know too many details, but I need to get to her."

"Oh, my God, Rina! What happened?"

"I am not sure, but I am praying she is fine."

I did not want to talk anymore about it since Gwen would get even more worried that Harold didn't give me any information about my daughter. I had tried to call him again, but he hadn't even answered his phone. For years, I put up with his bullshit because I felt that's what I was supposed to do. But now, I was tired.

"Sis, you know I have your back. You have always been that for me, and I blamed you for a lot that you couldn't control." Gwen's voice was shaking as she continued. "Last night, I realized that I have leaned on you for so long. I felt like there were times you owed me because you didn't stop bad things from happening. But that wasn't your responsibility."

"Gwen, you know I'm always there for you and will always be here," I said, startled that Gwen was telling me this. For so long, I felt Gwen took advantage of me because she knew she could count on me. From childhood until now, I had been there to bail Gwen out of her many crazy predicaments.

"I know, Rina, but I'm not always accountable for my actions. I have made you pay for things that you had no idea about."

Gwen stopped talking and stared out of the window. I waited for her to finish.

Her voice quivered. "I made a mess of my life, Rina. I spent so long looking for love that I did not realize the love I had right in front of me. I wanted so bad to be loved by a man that being loved by my kids, and even you were not enough. This weekend made me see that."

For the first time, I didn't know what to say to my little sister.

"Thank you for being there for me, Rina. And it wasn't your fault what happened when we were kids."

As much as I tried to stop my tears, one quietly slipped from the corner of my eye. I didn't know what would happen when we went to visit Mother Clara this weekend. But if nothing else, it seemed as if Gwen received something from us going. For that, I was grateful.

Chapter 34

Gwen

We pulled up at the Riverview Medical Center. Rina and I jumped out of the car. I was on Rina's heels as she ran to the admitting desk and asked for Mia's room number. I was oblivious to what was going on. Rina still had not filled me in on why exactly Mia was in the hospital, but I said a quick prayer that my niece would be all right.

The young fair-skinned nurse, with freckles all over her face at the desk, instructed us toward the elevator and up to the third floor. The elevators opened to Mia's floor. The first person we saw in the waiting room was Harold.

"Oh, my God, Harold! Is Mia okay?" Rina ran to him and hugged him.

Harold embraced her and assured her that Mia was fine. "She is awake, so you can go in and see her."

Harold had always been cool and calm, and today was no different. Once Rina let go of him and proceeded down the hall toward Mia's room, I gave Harold a quick hug and took a seat in the waiting room.

"I will give them some time alone," he said. "Gwen, you need anything?"

"No, I'm just praying Mia is going to be okay. What did the doctor say?"

"We all are praying that, and I will let Rina fill you in. I have to make a call. I'll be right back." Harold walked toward the elevator and pushed the down button.

I glanced at my brother-in-law and thought about how Rina was so lucky to have him. Coming from where we did, her life was picture perfect. I wanted that more than anything.

I just wanted to feel one moment of a man really caring about me the way Harold did for Rina. These thoughts crowded my mind, and I almost didn't hear my phone beeping.

I looked at my phone and smiled as a text message from Billy flashed on the screen.

"Hey, pretty lady, did y'all make it back safely?"

I didn't realize I was smiling so hard at my phone until I glanced up and noticed an older white lady sitting across from me in the waiting room, staring. She frowned once she caught me looking at her and then looked back down at the magazine she held in her hands.

I quickly responded to Billy's text.

"Yes, we made it. Thanks for checking on me."

I placed my phone on my lap and tried to hide my goofy grin. Seconds later, my phone beeped again, alerting me to another text.

"Okay, please call me when you can."

Before I had a chance to respond, Rina walked into the waiting room. Again, I noticed the difference in my sister's appearance.

The slim-fitting black pants she had on were a size too big, and her blouse hung loosely off her shoulders. She had aged years in a few days.

"Where did Harold go?" she asked, looking around the room. She frantically searched for him and even walked back outside to see if he was in the hallway. She walked back into the waiting room but continually looked over her shoulder for him.

"Oh, he had to make a call. How is Mia doing? What happened?"

"She is resting. The doctors said it was an anxiety attack," Rina informed me, still glancing out in the hallway for Harold.

I sighed with relief. "That girl is just like you, will work herself to death. I'm glad it was nothing serious. Can I go peek in on her?"

"The doctor says she needs her rest," Rina replied, finally sitting down beside me. "How long has Harold been gone?"

"Probably just a few minutes."

"Okay, just take my car on home. I will get Harold to bring me some clothes. I am going to spend the night here tonight." Rina handed me her car keys.

"Okay, Sis, let me know if y'all need anything. I will call you this evening to check on you."

I stood and hugged Rina before walking to the elevators. My phone beeped again with another text. Hoping it was Billy again, I frowned when a different name popped up on my screen. *Nope, not tonight*, I thought. I ignored the text from Chris saying that he really needed to talk to me.

•••

"Mr. Billy, you knew my momma when she was little like me?" Jaden, my youngest son, asked. He stood directly in front of Billy as if he were sizing him up. Jaden was only eleven, yet he was the most fearless out of my three boys.

"Why, yes, I did, young man," Billy replied, smiling at Jaden.

"D, please take your brothers to the movies," I told Deshawn, my oldest son.

We had just finished having dinner. Although I was nervous about Billy meeting my boys so soon, especially since this was his first time coming to see me, he insisted and wouldn't take no for an answer. However, now that we were all sitting in my living room after dinner, I realized this had been one of the best evenings I'd had in an awfully long time.

I handed Deshawn some money and watched my three boys walk out of the door, leaving Billy and me by ourselves.

"You really have some good young men," Billy said, smiling at me.

I was still in shock that William Dillard was now sitting beside me in my apartment on my sofa, smelling of Creed cologne and looking just as fine as he did when we were teenagers.

Billy was in his fifties now, and he didn't look a day over thirty. His bald head glistened in my dimly lit living room light. I had to do everything I possibly could to remain calm beside him. A button-up mint green shirt, and dark rinse blue jeans covered his slim muscular frame and made me stare at him even more now that we were by ourselves.

"Would you like some wine?" I asked, fighting apprehension. I wasn't sure what would take place now that we were alone. Just being in Billy's presence made me feel like an adolescent school girl with her first crush, which just happened to actually be.

"Yes, please."

I went into the kitchen, poured two glasses of Merlot, and brought them back into the living room. Noticing my uneasiness, Billy took one glass out of my shaking hands.

"Sit down, please." Billy lightly patted the space beside him on the couch.

Even though I made sure I dressed as sexy as I could tonight without having all my extra meat exposed, I still tugged on my black peplum shirt and pulled my gray pencil skirt up a little higher around my waist.

"As I talked to your boys tonight, I wondered if our child would have been a boy or a girl," Billy said, looking at me. His stare caused me to turn and gaze at the floor.

"I...I wonder that, too," I whispered.

Billy grabbed my hands like when we were at Mother Clara's house and held them. We didn't say a word. We sat in silence and thought about our baby. The baby that had been made in one night of young love.

Billy broke our silence with a tender kiss on my cheek. I looked at this gorgeous man who had stolen my heart as an adolescent and kissed him back on his lips. He took over my mouth and gave me one of the most passionate kisses I had ever experienced.

"Gwen, I never stopped loving you," he whispered into my ears.

"I still love you, too."

I stopped kissing him and stood up from the couch.

"Is everything okay?" Billy asked, sounding puzzled.

I grabbed his hand and pulled him up from the couch. "Just follow me," I commanded.

I led him down the hallway to my bedroom and stopped before I came to the door. I turned around and looked at the man who had my heart as a child and still had it to this day.

"Are you sure?" Billy asked as if we were teenagers again.

I didn't answer him but instead, pulled him into my room and led him to the bed. Thinking that I was going to show him exactly how I had longed for him over thirty years, I was shocked when he suddenly stopped me.

"Is everything okay?" I nervously asked. I pulled my shirt back down that had traveled up near my shoulders during us kissing.

"Yes, but let me show you just how lovely you are."

Billy unzipped my skirt and watched as it fell to my ankles. "Lie down," he ordered.

I did as I was told and waited for further instructions.

Billy removed my lace thongs and opened my legs. Anxiety swept over me, causing my legs to shake.

"Gwen, you are and have always been beautiful. Don't you ever forget that." Billy looked at me until I nodded that I would remember what he just said.

"Relax baby," Billy said before burying his head between my legs.

And for the first night in forever, I felt just as Bill saw me. Absolutely beautiful.

Chapter 35

Beatrice

"Can I please get some help?" I cried out for the third time. By now, I felt like I was being ignored, and the pain I was suffering was becoming too much to bear.

Melissa, my night nurse, had been into my room twice and offered no real assistance for the pain I was in. She sauntered in, drenched in a ton of blue eyeshadow and red lipstick, dropped two pills on the nightstand, and strolled out like I was not in a mountain of discomfort. Of all the times that I had been in rehab, this had to be the worst yet. Maybe I should not have gotten high with Ed the night before coming here. At first, all he had was weed. But after fucking his brains out, he made a few calls and got me exactly what I needed.

I felt like I was going to throw up for the second time today. There had to be something they could give me for the stomach pain and nausea I was experiencing.

As I was about to yell again, my door opened, and the sweetest voice silenced my cry.

"Beatrice, are you okay?" Vanessa asked, walking toward my bed.

I was balled up in the fetal position on my bed, rocking. I glanced up at her and, once I saw the concern written all over her face, could not help but smile. Her golden-brown tresses were tightly curled as if she had just gotten her hair done, and her delightful scent arrived at my bed before she did. With her being in the room, I immediately felt somewhat better.

"Beatrice, have they given you something for the pain?" she asked, checking my chart.

I groaned. "Not in a few hours," I lied. Although I did not want to deceive Vanessa, I could not take feeling so ill any longer. I needed more medicine now.

Vanessa walked over to the bed and placed her hand on my head. "You feel a little warm."

She gently touched my cheek, and I began to feel better. Usually, I was much more guarded with people. But all my defenses were down, and I needed her. I wanted her to make this wretched pain disappear. I was still shaking and hot, but Vanessa's calm aura began to soothe and relax me.

"You know, I've been taking care of Ms. Clara for the last two years, and she spoke about you and your mother often."

Between the pain and not really knowing how to respond to Vanessa, I decided to remain quiet and listen.

"My grandmother was a lot like Ms. Clara, very stern and controlling. But I knew she loved me, just like Ms. Clara loves you and your sisters."

I could tell Vanessa was only a few years younger than me. Yet, she had such an old soul, as the elders would say.

"Just relax and try to get some rest," she said, stroking my back.

As Vanessa continued to talk, I felt myself drifting to sleep. She didn't give me any more pills, but her presence was enough to ease some of my distress. It had been days since I was able to sleep. I could tell my body was thankful for the rest.

•••

"No, please. Someone, please," I cried. Alone in my dark closet, I struggled to breathe as the walls closed in on me. I heard Ruth Ann call my name, but I could not get out.

"Mom, where are you?" I cried. "Please, help, please."

But just like all the other times before, no one could save me. No one would come to rescue me, and I was stuck…stuck in my tiny closet. Afraid to leave and too scared to stay.

"Beatrice, wake up, Beatrice." I felt someone gently shaking my arm. "It's okay, wake up."

I glanced around the room and remembered where I was. Vanessa stood beside my bed, still calling my name.

"I'm fine," I told Vanessa, who had sat beside me on the bed.

The dream of me being young and hiding in my closet rolled around in my head. It had been years since I had that dream, and now it was all coming back to me.

"You want to talk about it?" Vanessa asked, rubbing my hand, and calming me down again. Her green scrubs snugged her frame, making it hard to look away. Again, her beauty had me in a trance.

"Beatrice?"

I snapped out of the spell Vanessa had cast on me. "When I was little, I always used to hide in the closet when my parents fought," I began.

As I told Vanessa about the rest of my dream, she slid closer to me on the bed.

"They say dreams often represent deeper meanings," Vanessa said, still rubbing my hand.

Just like earlier that day, I felt a sense of comfort with Vanessa. I thought about all the times I was locked in my closet and how I felt when I was inside. Now that I was completely sober, my mind was much clearer.

In my last group therapy session, the counselors shared some ways we could identify how we were feeling and the effect our past had on us.

"There were a lot of things I guess I kept hidden or hid in the closet like when I was young."

"What do you think was the biggest thing that you hid or was afraid to show?" Vanessa asked, her hand now resting on my leg. She looked at me as if she were begging me to tell my story. Tell her what was real to me, and my fears.

All my life, I was taught not to trust anyone or let people get too close to me. In all my relationships, I never let my guard down, and they all failed. I was in rehab now because I had even failed myself.

I looked at Vanessa as she waited for my answer. For the first time, with a clear mind, I was able to tell my truth.

I leaned over and placed my hand on top of Vanessa's hand that was still on my leg. Before she could say anything, I slid as close as I could to her, breathed in her captivating scent, and rested my lips on hers, answering her question.

Chapter 36

ClaRina

I had been lying to Gwen all these years about my marriage. I just added the real reason Mia was in the hospital to that list. I watched Mia sleeping peacefully; I grabbed the remote from the end of her bed and turned the television off. This was my third night in the hospital with her. I felt like climbing in the bed and checking myself in as well. I was still fatigued and dozing just as much as Mia.

"Mom?"

"Yes, baby," I said, moving over to the side of her bed. Mia's eye was still blackish purple and swollen. Her face was also enlarged and puffy. She groaned and shifted from her right side to her left. Her right arm was in a cast, and bandages were wrapped tightly underneath her breasts and the upper part of her stomach. Every time I looked at my daughter, a twinge of pain and regret ran through my body.

"How are you feeling, baby?" I asked, running my fingers through her short natural cut. I was glad she had finally taken out that dry weave she had been sporting for weeks.

"A little better. Has Maurice called?"

I rolled my eyes at the thought of Mia's boyfriend but resisted the urge to raise my voice and go off like I had done when I found out he was the reason Mia was here in the first place. I wanted to press charges. But Mia made it clear that she would never speak to me again if I went through with it. I did not want to lose my daughter at the time that she needed me the most.

I studied Mia, lying in bed, riddled in pain, and saw myself. I had hidden black eyes and bruises for so many years that it became second nature.

After a night where Harold had used me as his own personal punching bag, foundation and concealer were my best friends. Did I teach her that it was okay for a man to hit her? Did she think that this was love because of me?

"No, baby, just rest," I said. I thought back on all the times I had covered for Harold. When she was younger, Mia constantly asked when Daddy was coming home. I always made excuses for him. I made up lies like he was at work or on a business trip and gave her everything she wanted to take her mind off the fact that he was seldom around.

Thankfully, Maurice had not tried to come see her while she was at the hospital. I was convinced that had to do with Harold. Ironically, he wanted to kill Maurice for putting his hands on his child, but he continuously put his hands on his own wife.

Mia finally opened her eyes, "Ma, you don't look so good."

"Mia, I am fine. Just haven't gotten much sleep the last few nights. I've been too worried about you," I said, pulling the covers back over her.

"No, Ma, seriously. You look awful. Did you ever make an appointment like you said?"

I walked toward the sink and glanced in the mirror. My hair was matted down on my head, and I had deep bags under my eyes. My skin, usually vibrantly clear, held a disturbing darker tint. It was almost as if my face was dirty, and I needed to wash it. Mia was right. I looked like hell. Mother Clara's words echoed in my head. She kept repeating for me to go to the doctor.

Over the last few days, the dizzy spells had been worse, and I had zero energy. But as a mother, I knew I needed to take care of Mia and not focus on myself. However, since I refused to go home as long as Mia was in the hospital, I might as well see the doctor.

"Baby, I will make an appointment with the doctor tomorrow, I promise. Just get some rest."

Mia closed her eyes and drifted back to sleep. I sat down in the chair right across from her bed and watched her like I had for the last two nights. *How did I ever allow this to happen?* I thought.

•••

"Mrs. Faulk, how long have you been feeling lightheaded and dizzy?" Dr. Gaston glanced at me and then back down at his computer. His wrinkled beige fingers pecked at the letters as if he were in a beginner keyboarding class. "This new system they have us working in is just ridiculous," he huffed, rubbing his bald head.

I ignored his frustrated remark and tried to remember when I had my first dizzy spell. "For a few months now, off and on."

I was annoyed that this visit was taking so long and keeping me away from Mia. Even though the appointment was in the doctor's office connected to the hospital, I still did not want to leave her alone for much longer.

"Okay, we are going to draw blood and run a few tests. I will give you something that's gonna help with the dizziness. Your bloodwork should be back in a few days, and we'll go from there."

"Thank you so much, Doctor. I'm sure this is just age-related." I shook Dr. Gaston's hand and forced a fake smile. The fact that Mother Clara had stressed about me going to the doctor along with everyone else was causing anxiety I was desperately trying to suppress.

"Let's just be on the safe side and check everything." Dr. Gaston stood and walked toward the door. "Just rest and take the medicine. It's imperative that you take it easy and not overextend yourself."

"Yes, sir."

Dr. Gaston exited the room, and I put my clothes back on. I reached for my phone to call Harold and let him know how my appointment had gone. With everything that was going on, I didn't even remember to tell him I had scheduled a doctor's visit.

I dialed his number. After not getting his voicemail, I decided to try again.

"Harold?" I asked once the phone connected, but no one said anything.

I heard a woman laughing in the background. "Harold?" I asked, again louder. It was the middle of the day, and he was supposed to be at work. I could feel my blood pressure rising. I immediately began to get heated.

"Hey, Rina, is something wrong?" Harold asked.

"Where are you?" I demanded.

"Rina, what is the problem?"

"Never mind. Just continue to do what you were doing." I hung up the phone and waited a few seconds to see if he would call me back. The phone never rang.

As the days went on and years continued, I was growing more tired of our "agreement." He benefited from it; I just ended up deserted and trying to fill a void. Now that Mia was walking in my shoes, I felt more responsible for the way her life was going. Something had to give, and it had to be soon.

Chapter 37

Gwen

The last time I felt this much joy had to be the first night Billy and I were together. I turned on my side and stared at the man who had given me so much happiness in a few weeks.

"Are you looking at me while I sleep?" Billy opened one eye and peeked at me.

"I guess you can say that, Mr. Dillard." I laughed and leaned in to kiss his cheek. Before I was able to place a peck on his bearded face, he turned his head, grabbed me, and pulled me on top of him.

"I love you, Gwendolyn Kendall."

"And I love you, William 'Billy' Dillard."

This time when Billy kissed me, I was not consumed with the loss of our child. The pain would always be there, but it did not control me like it had done for so many years.

•••

Mother Clara passed away on a sun-drenched Friday morning. Since the current sunrise was so pleasant, the day was too lovely to think about someone transitioning to a better place. I imagined Mother Clara at peace now that she had made amends with my sisters and me. She died almost a month and a half after we went to visit her. I had heard that people could wait until they see someone special, or that meant a lot to them before they died. I felt like this may have held true for Mother Clara.

"How are you feeling?" Billy asked, stirring a pot of grits, standing in my kitchen. Billy had come to visit last night and was here when Vanessa called to tell me that Mother Clara had died.

"I'm not sure," I said, sitting down at the table. "I haven't forgiven Mother for what she did, but I don't want to keep holding on to it."

"Maybe you should talk to someone about it," Billy suggested. "I thought about doing that, too, myself."

"What, like a therapist?" I asked. I was slightly offended Billy thought I needed to seek help.

"Calm down, Gwen," I was only suggesting it because of everything you have been through."

"I don't think I need to sit on someone's couch that don't even know me and tell them all my deep dark feelings." I rolled my eyes at Billy and stood up from the table.

Billy placed the lid on the pot of grits and walked toward me. I turned my back to him. I didn't want to talk anymore about seeing a therapist.

"You know why I love you so much?" he asked, standing behind me and wrapping his arms around me.

I shrugged my shoulders, still not wanting to talk to him. I already had a hard time talking about my past to Rina, who went through my childhood with me, therefore, talking to a stranger about it was a definitive no.

Billy turned me around so that I would face him. "Your strength is what I love so much about you. I know what that house did to you. I know what losing our baby did to you. But you still wake up every morning with a smile on your face and take care of your boys. I just want you to love you as much as I do."

As his words sunk in, I thought about what Mother Clara had told me before she died. She also wanted me to start loving myself.

I thought for a minute, and maybe Billy was right. I had made so many bad mistakes in the past because of the things I had gone through as a child that it wouldn't hurt to try and get help. Now that Billy was back in my life, I surely did not want to do anything to mess up this new happiness I was experiencing.

As if he heard my thoughts, Billy pulled me into him and squeezed me tightly. "We can do this together. You will not be alone."

For the first time, I was thankful Rina had made me go to Timmonsville with her. Finally, something good had happened when I went back to the house that had almost destroyed me.

Chapter 38

Beatrice

A New Day Rehabilitation Center had been my home for over a month now. I was finally feeling completely better. Although the original plan had been to stay for only a month, I felt like I needed the extra time here. The walls had stopped closing in on me, and I had not had any more nightmares of when I was a child. I didn't realize how much I had been holding in. I wanted, more than anything, to be free of that. It felt as if a ton of bricks had been lifted off me. I was able to exhale and just breathe. I felt set free.

My initial reason for wanting to come see Mother Clara was just to get her money. But as time went by and the longer I dealt with myself, I realized I needed to come see her. Visiting Mother Clara helped me more than I had ever imagined it would.

"Are you ready to go?" Vanessa asked, zipping up my duffle bag. With a golden headband placed on top of her head, she mimicked a goddess. My queen. My beauty.

I smiled and walked toward her. Never had I met someone I felt like I could trust and be myself with. Never did I even want to have faith in anyone. It was second nature for me to turn away from people and automatically distrust them, but Vanessa was different. So many nights, she had sat up with me and held my hand. This stint in rehab was unlike the rest because I was forced to be honest with myself. I was in a town where I had no one and, with Vanessa's help, I faced my truth. She was my light at the end of a never-ending tunnel. The first night we kissed, Vanessa shared that Mother Clara told her that I needed her. She said she thought it was only because of my drug habit. But when we met, she saw in my eyes that it was more.

"Ms. Clara is proud." Vanessa placed her arms around me and delicately hugged me. I closed my eyes, taking in her sweet citrus smell, and allowed her to comfort me. Vanessa had been with Mother Clara the previous night and informed me that she had passed this morning.

Shockingly, her death affected me more than I thought it would. Granted, I had just gotten to know Mother Clara, but she had done more for me in a few weeks than anyone had done for me in my life.

"Thank you." I lifted my head from Vanessa's shoulder and gave her a simple peck on the lips. She had been my saving grace. I proudly stepped out of my closet and embraced the person I had hidden for so long.

•••

I entered Mother Clara's house, and a serene feeling poured over me. Before my stay at the rehab center, my few days spent at this house meant nothing to me. I was so wrapped up in just getting money from Mother Clara that I had not noticed all of the photographs of my family that decorated the walls and tables in the living room. I never wanted to know the people in these pictures, but now I did. I wanted to know and understand my family—*my family*.

I gazed at the different photos and studied each one.

"Now that you will be living here, I can tell you who everyone is," Vanessa stated from behind me, reading my thoughts.

"I would love that. I can't believe she left me this house and the money she promised."

"She knew you would do right by yourself, your mother, and her." Vanessa put her arm around my waist and snuggled up close to me. "And I am going to put some meat on your bones, too." She giggled.

I took in a deep breath and exhaled. I couldn't recall if I had ever felt this way, but I was content. I was at peace.

Chapter 39

ClaRina

I turned over in the guest bed I had been staying in the last month and stared at the wall. One month had passed since I'd received my test results, and I was still in disbelief. Dr. Gaston made me come in for a visit instead of providing me with the results over the phone. Once he told me what my ailment was, I asked him at least four times if he was sure.

His words rolled around in my head again. I tried to sit up in the bed, but even that was difficult. No matter how much sleep I got, every day, I grew more tired. I thought about the pistol that sat in the top of my closet and was tempted to use it to go ahead and end whatever days I had left on this earth. However, Mia needed me. That thought alone kept me from putting the gun to my head and pulling the trigger.

My phone beeped like it had been doing all morning. I had ignored it for the past few days, but I decided to check my messages this morning. I was not shocked when I saw five messages from Gwen and two from Beatrice.

My mind went back to the doctor's words, "Mrs. Faulk, you are HIV positive."

Mother Clara stressed that I needed to go to the doctor, and now I knew why. She was aware that there was a chance I had contracted this deadly disease from Uncle Dale. She knew and waited to tell me. She knew, and now she was gone.

I laid back down and turned on my side, trying to go back to sleep. It was a struggle just to get some rest. However, the sleeping medicine Dr. Gaston had given me was allowing me to nap for a few hours at a time.

"Rina, you up?" Harold asked before opening the door.

The only thing I had told him was that I had pneumonia and needed to stay in the guestroom until I was better. He was so wrapped up in his little mistress that it really did not matter to him if he saw me or not.

"How are you feeling, baby?" Harold asked, sitting beside me on the bed and placing his hand on my forehead. His Polo cologne that used to draw me into him just made me queasy now.

"Not that much better."

There was no way I was going to tell Harold that the doctor had informed me of my diagnosis. I could not speak those words to myself, much less to him. If spoken aloud, that would make it real, and I was sure I would wake up from this nightmare at any moment.

"Mia said she called to check on you but couldn't reach you." Harold glanced over at the nightstand where my cell phone was.

"How is she?" I asked, trying to change the subject.

"Doing better, she is almost 100 percent now. But there is something else I need to tell you." Harold paused for a moment. He looked at me and then glanced down at the floor.

"Yes?" I asked, trying to push myself up into a sitting position.

"Ebony is pregnant again."

I stared at Harold. My husband of thirty years was once again telling me that his mistress was pregnant with their third child. After his second child with her, my husband had promised me that there would be no more: my husband, the adulterer, and liar.

"Harold."

As soon as I said his name, I saw his demeanor change. "I didn't have to tell you, but I did. So, deal with it. Ebony is pregnant, and I can't change that." Harold stood and walked toward the door. "I won't be here tonight or tomorrow. If you need something, just call."

I remained silent and watched Harold walk out of the door. My life was such a fucking joke. I laid back down and wished I was already dead.

•••

I finally was beginning to feel a little better and actually had an appetite. I even felt like putting on real clothes. I dressed in a pair of pinstriped pants and a yellow blouse and headed to get my prescription filled that the doctor had given me over two weeks ago. Harold had been gone for a day. I did not anticipate him returning anytime soon, which was completely fine with me.

I dialed Mia's number and waited for her to answer.

The voicemail picked up. I decided not to leave a message. If I were still feeling better tomorrow, I would go by and see her.

I stared at the bottle of pills on the counter and thought again about all the information the doctor had given me. There was a chance for me to live a healthy life, thinking positively if I continuously took my medicine, but I felt I had been given a death sentence. I needed to tell Harold so he could get checked. But how would I inform him of that? I picked up my phone again to call Gwen.

As I was dialing her number, Harold unlocked the front door and staggered in. I did not expect him to come back tonight. I was looking forward to having a night to myself to figure out my next move.

"I see you're feeling better," Harold said, standing in front of me. I smelled the whiskey on his breath. His tie loosely hung around his neck, and the top two buttons of his ash gray dress shirt were loose.

I took a few steps back to widen the distance between us. "Yeah, just a little bit."

"Good because I want you tonight." Harold came closer to me and reached for me.

"Not tonight, Harold. I am still contagious," I said, thinking about how deadly I really was.

"Rina, I don't give a shit about that! I need you. Ebony is not feeling good and has been having morning sickness. I want you now."

Harold lunged toward me and grabbed my arm. "Let go!" I screamed.

I tried to yank away from him, but he had a tight grip on me. "Harold, I am not playing. I don't give a damn about your mistress! Let me go!" I insisted again.

Harold pulled me to him and kissed me rough. He placed his free hand around my neck.

I looked at him and, at that moment, saw Uncle Dale.

•••

I was a hypocrite. Hypocrisy flowed through my body as if it were the only substance that willed me to stay alive. It seeped through my pores with every breath I took and erupted from my mouth with every word that passed between my lips. My name should have been ClaRina Hypocrite Kendall Faulk since that one word represented my entire existence and was exactly what had brought me to this moment. I sucked in two quick breaths and slowly exhaled to slow down my rapidly beating heart. Lifting my shaking hand, I rubbed my eyes, smearing fresh warm blood all over the right side of my face. Sweat dripped from my new pixie cut and found its way to the corners of my eyes. Between the mixing of body fluids, it was nearly impossible to see clearly. I was almost at the point of completely losing my mind, but now I was imagining things as well. I felt like the young boy in the movie, *The Sixth Sense*. His words crept from my mouth and were released as only a mere whisper, "I see dead people."

My living room was dark, except for the moonlight shining through the slits of my blinds. Glancing over to my right, which was the only dimly lit corner of the room, I hoped the person who had appeared had vanished just as quickly. However, I wasn't that lucky. She was as evident as the half-dead body that laid at my feet. Mother Clara sat in her once favorite wooden rocking chair calmly moving back and forth. Draped over her large body was the black and white striped housecoat we regularly saw her in as children. A blank expression was frozen on her face and her long gray hair, which was always pinned up in a bun, was in complete disarray. However, her confused demeanor wasn't what almost made my knees buckle. In my grandmother's lap rested a two-by-four. The large piece of lumber was drenched with blood dripping onto my hardwood floors.

"Mother Clara?" I asked whispering.

She didn't stop rocking, nor did she look at me. She didn't even pause to acknowledge my presence. The bright red liquid continued to steadily fall from the wood.

I attempted to call her name again, but the words were bound in my throat. My hands were soaked from the perspiration and blood. I wiped them on my blue pinstriped suit pants. But no matter how hard I tried, I couldn't get them clean.

"It's not going anywhere," a voice from the opposite side of my living room called out.

I peered through the darkness where the words had traveled from and saw her—my mother. Again, I was seeing dead people.

"Mom?" my voice was barely audible at this point.

She stood in the corner and smiled at me. She wore a simple black dress on her slender frame. As always, she looked beautiful and fancy. Her medium-length tresses were cut in a bob, and she looked peaceful. A peace that was not at all parallel to the mother I had known.

"Mom, is that really you? Ruth Ann?"

She smiled again. As her grin slowly transformed into a scowling frown, I noticed what was in her hand. She looked down, gripped the handle of a silver pistol, and then looked back up at me. I shook my head. My mind was playing tricks on me. The same gun she held in her hands was the exact gun I clutched in mine.

"You are me," my grandmother and mom said together.

"No!" I screamed, shaking my head, and dropping the pistol to the floor! "No, no, no!"

My grandmother stood from her chair and finally looked at me. She and my mom began to move toward me; Mother Clara with her bloody two-by-four and my mom with her gun. They pointed both objects at me.

"You are us," they said in unison.

Their words sent a chill through my body, and I couldn't stand up any longer. I fell to my knees, landing in a sea of blood.

"I'm not!" I cried out. "Please, God, I'm not like them," I pleaded as if the master above could hear me. Even if He could, I doubted He would pay my pleas any attention after what I had done.

"You are us," rang in my ears over and over again as I buried my face in my hands and cried.

Moments passed, and the room fell silent. My tears subsided. I looked around for my mother and grandmother, but they were now gone. The only person left in the room with me was Harold. My husband's lifeless body was lying on the floor in front of me. His head faced me, and fresh blood streamed from his mouth. His soulless eyes were still open and stared at me as if to ask why.

"Oh, God! I am them," I said as the realization of what I had done sunk in.

Just then, even though they were gone, I still heard the voices of the two women who just had stood in front of me. And since I was more like them than I ever wanted to admit, I would do exactly what they would have done at this moment.

I picked up my gun from the floor, regained just enough strength to point it at Harold and pulled the trigger once more.

"You were going to die anyway."

Epilogue

ClaRina

I folded the three-page letter from Gwen and placed it back in its envelope. I was pleasantly surprised to find out she was engaged to be married. Billy was the right man for her; he loved Gwen and the boys. I knew he would take good care of her. She did not need me anymore. Although I loved being there for my sister all these years, it was a weight off of me that she had someone else she could truly depend on.

I thought about both of my sisters and was extremely proud of them. Even though it had been close to a year since I had seen them, we often kept in touch. At my request, the weekly visits stopped. I wanted them to focus on their own lives and not mine. It was time for both my sisters to let go of the past and live and love unapologetically. From what they told me in their letters, they were doing just that. Beatrice and Vanessa were living together in Mother Clara's house, and the pictures of the renovations they had done were stunning. I would always be grateful for the weekend we spent together at Mother Clara's house. We now shared a bond that could never be broken.

"You have a visitor," Scotman announced as he passed by. He was one of the nicer guards in my area, always talking calmly and there were very few times I saw him using excessive force on anyone.

I was only able to see the back of him walking by, so I stood from my bed to see if he was talking to me. After a few seconds, he came back and repeated himself. "You have a visitor."

The doors clinked as they opened. Scotman led me down the hall to the visitation area. I smoothed out my clothes to make sure I was presentable for whoever had decided to visit me today. No one was on the visiting list, so I wondered who it could be.

I entered the large visitation room and saw Mia sitting alone at a table by the window. Her hair was pulled back into a high ponytail; her caramel skin was glowing. It had been so long since I had seen my daughter look as beautiful as she did today.

Mia pulled up her black V-neck dress so that not too much cleavage showed and smiled at me. "Hey, Mom. How you doing in here?" she asked.

"I'm okay, baby. Taking my meds and feeling pretty good today. You are glowing."

"There is a reason why, Mom," Mia said, still grinning from ear to ear. Her entire face was lit up with excitement. "I know I told you I would come this weekend to see you, but I just couldn't wait any longer to tell you the news."

I was slightly confused but dared not interrupt Mia. Whatever she wanted to tell me had to be important for her to drive four hours on a day she had to work.

"I'm pregnant, Mom!" Mia exclaimed, rubbing her belly.

I stared at Mia and then down at her stomach. "I'm going to be a grandmother?" I asked, feeling my eyes watering up.

"Yes, ma'am," Mia beamed.

Although I just wanted Mia to relish in her announcing the news to me, I had to ask her the one question I was sure would wipe the enthusiasm off her face.

"And how does Maurice feel about this?"

Mia hesitated for a moment. She reached across the table and grabbed my hands. "We are no longer together, and I have a protective order against him."

I let out a sigh of relief. "Are you happy, Mia?"

Her smile returned, "Yes, ma'am. I am. For years, I saw what Daddy did to you. I knew about his other children. I thought that was just how people loved one another. I believed that love was supposed to hurt."

As Mia continued, I felt a tightness in my throat. I loved my daughter. But all these years, I had been sending her the wrong message.

She watched her dad disrespect me on so many levels, and I had taught her that it was normal. Growing up, I had watched Grandpa Henry do the same to Mother Clara.

"Mom, I wish you weren't in here, but I understand. I loved Dad, but I hated what he did to you. I want you to know I love you, and I get it."

My eyes filled with tears as Mia increased her grip on my hands. I was proud of my daughter for getting out of a situation I was never strong enough to leave. She and my grandchild would be safe, and that was what I had prayed for.

"Mom, I know now that love isn't supposed to hurt. Me and my baby will be okay. The cycle ends here. And one day when you are out of this place, you will be able to hold your grandchild."

As I walked back to my cell, I thought about the last thing Mia had said. All the years that generational curses had plagued my family was finally coming to an end. Her words replayed over in my head. "The cycle ends here."